Leaning forwar

skimmed his knu

of her cheek. He

in her eyes.

Desire.

The same desire that was now throbbing insistently in his veins. For one small moment in time, he wasn't Trent Marlowe, child psychologist. He was just Trent Marlowe, a college student who was hopelessly, head-over-heels in love with a young woman he had known since the fourth grade.

And had wanted since the beginning of time.

Tilting his head, he softly brushed his lips against hers, half expecting Laurel to pull back.

But she didn't. She remained exactly where she was.

And kissed him back.

Dear Reader,

Welcome back to KATE'S BOYS, the saga that actually began more than twenty years ago when Bryan Marlowe hired yet another nanny for his four rambunctious sons, only to lose his heart to her.

Trent is the son who followed his stepmother, Kate, into the child psychology field. Warm and sensitive, he enjoys working with children. But he is in no way prepared for the woman who comes to him, begging that he help her son, Cody. "She" is the woman who, seven years earlier, vanished from his life after he proposed to her. Trent soon discovers that he doesn't have all the facts, not about Cody, and definitely not about Laurel Valentine. Reluctantly agreeing to take on her son as a patient, Trent begins a journey into self-awareness that will, in the end, leave none of them untouched.

Thank you for returning to read about Kate, one of my favorite heroines, and the family she came to mean so much to. As ever, from the bottom of my heart, I wish you someone to love who loves you back.

Marie Ferrarella

MARIE FERRARELLA

MISTLETOE AND MIRACLES

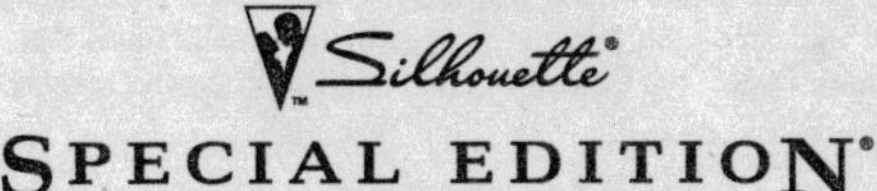

Published by Silhouette Books
America's Publisher of Contemporary Romance

Recycling programs for this product may not exist in your area.

ISBN-13: 978-0-373-24941-1
ISBN-10: 0-373-24941-1

MISTLETOE AND MIRACLES

This edition published by arrangement with Harlequin Books S.A.

Visit Silhouette Books at www.eHarlequin.com

Printed in U.S.A.

Books by Marie Ferrarella

Silhouette Special Edition

††*Her Good Fortune* #1665
‡*Because a Husband Is Forever* #1671
‡‡*The Measure of a Man* #1706
‡*She's Having a Baby* #1713
‡*Her Special Charm* #1726
Husbands and Other Strangers #1736
§*The Prodigal M.D. Returns* #1775
°*Mother in Training* #1785
Romancing the Teacher #1826
§§*Remodeling the Bachelor* #1845
§§*Taming the Playboy* #1856
§§*Capturing the Millionaire* #1863
°°*Falling for the M.D.* #1873
~*Diamond in the Rough* #1910
~*The Bride with No Name* #1917
~*Mistletoe and Miracles* #1941

Silhouette Romantic Suspense

**In Broad Daylight* #1315
**Alone in the Dark* #1327
**Dangerous Disguise* #1339
~~*The Heart of a Ruler* #1412
**The Woman Who Wasn't There* #1415
**Cavanaugh Watch* #1431
†*Her Lawman on Call* #1451
†*Diagnosis: Danger* #1460
***My Spy* #1472
†*Her Sworn Protector* #1491
**Cavanaugh Heat* #1499
†*A Doctor's Secret* #1503
†*Secret Agent Affair* #1511
**Protecting His Witness* #1515
+*Colton's Secret Service* #1528

*Cavanaugh Justice
~~Capturing the Crown
†The Doctors Pulaski
**Mission: Impassioned
††The Fortunes of Texas: Reunion
‡The Cameo
‡‡Most Likely To...
§The Alaskans
°Talk of the Neighborhood
§§The Sons of Lily Moreau
°°The Wilder Family
~Kate's Boys
+The Coltons: Family First

MARIE FERRARELLA

This *USA TODAY* bestselling and RITA® Award-winning author has written over one hundred and fifty novels for Silhouette Books, some under the name Marie Nicole. Her romances are beloved by fans worldwide. Visit her Web site at www.marieferrarella.com.

To
Hermine Katarina Hirsch,
who, according to her loving daughter, Terry,
is the best mother in the world.

Chapter One

For a moment, Trent Marlowe thought he was dreaming.

When he first looked up from the latest article on selective mutism and saw her standing in the doorway of his office, he was certain he had fallen asleep.

But even though the article was dry, the last time he'd actually nodded out while sitting at a desk had been during an eight-o'clock Pol-Sci 1 class, where the lackluster professor's monotone voice had been a first-class cure for insomnia.

He'd been a college freshman then.

And so had she.

Blinking, Trent glanced down at his appointment calendar and then up again at the sad-eyed, slender blonde. It was nine in the morning and he had a full day ahead of him, beginning with a new patient, a Cody Greer. Cody was only six years old and was brought in by his mother, Laurel Greer.

When he'd seen it on his schedule, the first name had given him a fleeting moment's pause. It made him remember another Laurel. Someone who had been a very important part of his life. But that was years ago and if he thought of her every now and then, it was never in this setting. Never walking into his office. After all, like his stepmother, he had become a child psychologist, and Laurel Valentine was hardly a child. Even when she'd been one.

Laurel wasn't that unusual a name. It had never occurred to him that Laurel Greer and Laurel Valentine were one and the same person.

And yet, here she was, in his doorway. Just as achingly beautiful as ever.

Maybe more so.

Trent didn't remember rising from behind his desk. Didn't remember opening his mouth to speak. His voice sounded almost surreal to his ear as he said her name. "Laurel?"

And then she smiled.

It was a tense, hesitant smile, but still Laurel's smile, splashing sunshine through the entire room. That was when he knew he wasn't dreaming, wasn't revisiting a space in his mind reserved for things that should have been but weren't.

Laurel remained where she was, as if she had doubts about taking this last step into his world. "Hello, Trent. How are you?"

Her voice was soft, melodic. His was stilted. "Startled."

He'd said the first word that came to him. But this wasn't a word association test. Trent laughed dryly to shake off the bewildered mood that closed around him.

How long had it been? Over seven years now. And, at first glance, she hadn't changed. She still had a shyness that made him think of a fairy-tale princess in need of rescue.

Confusion wove its way through the moment. Had she come here looking for him? Or was it his professional services she needed? But he didn't treat adults.

"I'm a child psychologist," he heard himself telling her.

Her smile widened, so did the radiance. But that could have just been a trick of the sunshine streaming in the window behind him.

"I know," she said. "I have a child."

Something twisted inside of him, but he forced himself to ignore it. Trent tilted his head slightly as he looked behind her, but there didn't seem to be anyone with Laurel, at least not close by. Trent raised an inquiring eyebrow as his eyes shifted back to her.

"He's at home," she explained. "With my mother."

He looked at his watch even though three minutes ago he'd known what time it was. Right now he wasn't sure of anything. The ground had opened up beneath him and he'd fallen down the rabbit hole.

"Shouldn't he be in school?"

Laurel sighed before answering, as if some burden had made her incredibly tired. "These days, he doesn't want to go anymore." Laurel pressed her lips together and looked at him hopefully. "Can I come in?"

Idiot, Trent berated himself. But the sight of his first, no, his *only* love after all these years had completely thrown him for a loop, incinerating his usual poise.

He forced himself to focus. To relax. With effort, he locked away the myriad questions popping up in his brain.

"Of course. Sorry. Seeing you just now really caught me off guard." He gestured toward the two chairs before his sleek, modern desk. "Please, take a seat."

She moved across the room like the model she had once confided she wanted to become, gliding gracefully into one of the chairs he'd indicated. Placing her purse on the floor beside her, she crossed her ankles and folded her hands in her lap.

She seemed uncomfortable and she'd never been ill at ease around him before. But there were seven years between then and now. A lot could have happened in that time.

"I wanted to talk to you about Cody before you started working with him, but I didn't want him to hear me."

Did she think the boy wouldn't understand? Or that Cody would understand all too well? "Why?"

"Cody's practically a statue as it is. I don't want him feeling that I'm talking about him as if he wasn't there. I mean…" She stopped abruptly, working her lower lip the way she used to when a topic was too hard for her to put into words. Some things didn't change. He wasn't sure if he found comfort in that or not.

When she looked up at him, he realized that she'd bitten

down on her lower lip to keep from crying. Tears shimmered in her eyes. "I don't know where to start."

"Anyplace that feels comfortable," he told her gently, a well of old feelings springing forth. He smiled at her encouragingly. "Most people start at the beginning."

No place feels comfortable, Laurel thought. She was hanging on by a thread and that thread was getting thinner and thinner. Any second now, she was going to fall into the abyss.

Clenching her hands together, she forced herself to rally. She couldn't fall apart, she couldn't. She had to save Cody. Or, more accurately, she had to get Trent to save Cody, because if anyone could help her son, it was Trent.

"He doesn't talk. Not a word since..." Despite her resolve, her voice cracked and then suddenly deserted her. A wave of déjà vu washed over her.

Trent was sorely tempted to come around to her side of the desk and take her hands into his, tempted to coax her up to her feet and just hold her until her strength returned and she could talk again.

That was what he would have done once.

But they weren't high school sweethearts anymore, weren't freshmen at college, planning on a future together. They'd separated and gone their own ways, pulled apart by baggage that she couldn't seem to unpack before him.

Well, she'd obviously unpacked that baggage for someone else, he thought, an unexpected shaft of bitterness pricking him. He banked it down. Laurel had gone on to marry and have a family. She wasn't the Laurel he still sometimes dreamed about.

The Laurel he'd once asked to marry him—just before she had disappeared.

The best he could do was round the desk and sit down in the chair beside her, the very act cutting into the professional air that was supposed to exist between them. But that was all right. Now that he knew whose son Cody was, he wouldn't take the case. He'd be too close to it.

But he could definitely help her pull her thoughts together so that he could refer the boy to either his mother or one of the two other psychologists who shared the suite with him.

"Since?" he coaxed.

Laurel squared her shoulders, as if bracing herself against the next words she was about to say. "Since his father died."

"I'm sorry for your loss," he murmured. Trent glanced down at her hand and saw that she still wore a wedding ring. "How recently?"

"Almost a year," she whispered.

A year. Most women would have moved on by now, encouraged by their family or friends to meet life head-on. But then, Laurel had never been like most women.

Taking a breath, she appeared to regain some control over herself. The old Laurel would have gone to pieces first, then, after a while, struggled to rebuild herself. There had been changes after all, he thought, with distant admiration.

"It was a car accident." She was squeezing her hands together so tightly her knuckles were white. "Cody was with him."

Because he'd lost his mother at a very young age, the empathy Trent felt was immediate, opening a distant door inside him. She had died in a plane crash and it had haunted him and made attachments very difficult for him. He could only imagine how much worse it would have been to have watched life ebb away from her. "He saw his father die?"

"Yes." Laurel's voice was hoarse. "Cody was in the car for almost an hour while the fire department tried to get him out." Cody and Matt had been on their way to a campsite. She'd wanted to come, but Matt had told her to stay home, that he had wanted to spend some time alone with Cody, and she had reluctantly agreed. She still couldn't shake the feeling that if she'd been there, things might have gone differently. "When I got to the hospital, I expected Cody to be hysterical, crying, something. But there was nothing. No emotion at all. It was as if his body had remained and the rest of him had just gone away.

"At first, I thought it was shock, that it would wear off, but…" She looked up at Trent helplessly. "It hasn't. He hasn't said a single word."

"Have you had him checked out physically?"

"What kind of a mother do you think I am?" A tiny spark of anger flared in her eyes and he was glad of it. Anger helped people survive situations that would have otherwise crushed them. "Of course I had him checked out.

I took him to a pediatrician, then another pediatrician, then a neurologist and finally to our family doctor." The kindly man had been her last hope. "There's nothing physically wrong with Cody." She took another deep breath. "Dr. Miller suggested I try a child psychologist. He gave me your name."

He knew a Dr. Miller. The man was on the staff of Blair Memorial, but he couldn't recall that he had ever particularly impressed the physician. "My name?" he questioned.

"Well, your office's name," Laurel amended with a small shrug, as if it were all one and the same. "But when I saw your name on the referral card he gave me..."

His name had jumped up at her and her heart had all but stopped. For the first time in months, she'd started to think that there was hope for Cody. She raised her eyes to Trent's. "I remembered how kind you could be, how patient."

"Laurel—"

He was going to turn her down, she could tell by the tone of his voice. And he had every right to, because of what she'd done. But desperation made her cut him off. She began talking more quickly. For Cody's sake.

"Trent, he was the brightest boy. Outgoing, friendly, smart." Her heart almost broke when she thought of the way things used to be. "He could read when he was four. I know this was a huge trauma for him. He loved his dad and this just devastated him. But you can find a way to get through to him, I *know* you can."

Everything told Trent to walk away. Everything but the

look in her eyes. Still, it wouldn't be right. He tried to make her understand why he was turning her down—or trying to. "I really don't think that I'm the right person to treat him."

She wasn't going to take no for an answer, she wasn't. Trent was her son's last hope. "Because of our past history?"

There it was in a nutshell. Trent made no attempt to deny it. "Yes."

She refused to accept that. She *had* to make him understand. "But that's exactly what makes you so right. Because I know you have this way about you, of drawing people out." Laurel didn't want to get into specifics, it was too painful for her. But she would if she had to. This wasn't about her, it was about her son and she would do anything to save him, to pluck him out of the living hell he was in. "I don't trust people very readily."

"I remember." It had been hard, getting her to finally open up, to tell him what haunted her. But ultimately, even knowing hadn't helped. If anything, it had made her leave. Because he knew. It was the only excuse he could think of for her abrupt departure from his life.

"But I trust you," she continued. The vulnerability in her voice wove its way under his skin, into his very soul. "Trent, I've tried everything to make him speak. I got him a special tutor to help him keep up. But his grades just kept dropping off. Kids make fun of him and I can literally *see* him going further and further into his shell." She slid onto the edge of the chair, her body rigid with fear. "I don't know what to do anymore. I can't lose him, Trent. He's such a special little boy and he's so helpless."

Laurel paused, as if debating whether or not to tell him more. Taking a breath, she made her decision and plunged in. "I caught him playing with matches the other day. He *knows* better than that." Her eyes held his, pleading for his help. "I'm afraid that he's really going to hurt himself if something doesn't happen to pull him out of this."

Trent watched her for a long moment. He should stick to his principles and refer her to Lucas Andrews, whose technique was similar to his, or even to his stepmother. Kate Llewellyn Marlowe could make anyone open up. She had worked wonders on all four of them when she'd come into their lives as their nanny more than twenty years ago. And along the way, she'd even changed his father, making him more human.

Everything he'd ever learned about patience and love had come from Kate, as had mending broken souls. It was for the best if Laurel took her son to either of them. But it was hard saying no to the expression in Laurel's eyes. There was a part of him that still loved her after all this time, even though he'd made his peace and accepted the way things had turned out a long time ago.

Or so he had told himself.

He supposed it wouldn't do any harm to ask questions, find out a few things and get them out of the way.

"What does Cody do with his time?" Trent asked. "Does he play with other children?"

Laurel shook her head. "Not anymore. Not even his

best friend, Scott, who stuck by him when the other kids started to tease him. He used to be so sociable, so outgoing. To see him now…" She pressed her lips together again, shaking her head.

"Then how does he spend his time?" Trent asked. "Does he watch television all the time? Stare off into space? What does he do?"

"He plays video games," she told him, a sad smile playing on her lips. At least that was preferable to doing nothing, she supposed. "Actually, it's more like one video game. It involves race cars—his father got it for him." She couldn't bring herself to take the game away from Cody, even though watching him play worried her. "He crashes the cars over and over again. And he plays with his toy cars." Her voice grew shaky. "He stages car crashes with them—"

"Destroying what destroyed his father," Trent commented.

"In essence, yes." And then she surprised him by suddenly leaning forward and taking his hand in both of hers. "Trent, please," she begged. "Please help him."

For a moment, logic warred with emotion. He knew what he should say, knew what he should do. But it was a short-lived battle. Because this was Laurel and she had been through so much in her life. He couldn't be the reason she lost all hope.

"All right, I'll see him—at least to evaluate him," he qualified. "Bring him in." Flipping a page, Trent glanced at his calendar. He had an opening. "Tomorrow morning at nine good for you?"

Tears rose in her eyes again, this time from gratitude.

"Anytime is good for me," Laurel told him with relief. "Oh, God." Her voice almost gave out as she whispered, "Thank you, Trent."

"Don't thank me yet," Trent warned. "I haven't done anything."

"But you will." There was no doubt in her mind that he would help Cody, that he would find a way to make the boy better, return him to his former self.

"This isn't a magic act, Laurel. I can't just pass a wand over him and suddenly make him better. This might take a great deal of time." Even as he said it, he couldn't help wondering if he was up to it. If he was biting off more than he could chew. Which was crueler? To offer no hope or false hope? Right now he couldn't honestly say.

"You made me better," she recalled, then amended, "Almost."

Many small moments flooded his mind, moments that they had shared together. Moments that had once made him believe they would always be together. But things hadn't turned out that way.

"It's the 'almost' that trips you up every time," he commented, squelching a wave of sadness that threatened to wash over him.

And then he looked at her for a long moment. She was a beautiful woman. She always had been, right from the beginning. And, from the sound of it, she'd gone through a great deal in the last year. She'd never had it easy. She was fragile, but she was still here. That spoke well for her resilience.

"How are *you* doing?" he asked softly.

She seemed surprised by the question. "I'm fine," Laurel said a bit too quickly. That same sad smile played on her lips. "Except that I'm really worried about Cody."

"But aside from that?" he urged. There had been a time when she talked to him, as much as she had talked to anyone.

She raised her head, a curtain falling into place. "Fine. I'm fine."

It seemed that Cody wasn't the only one who'd withdrawn from the world. In her own way, she had, too. But that was a conversation for another time. Maybe.

"Well, I've taken up enough of your time." She picked up her purse, opening it on her lap and taking out her checkbook. "So, how much do I owe you?"

Trent shook his head. "This wasn't a session, Laurel."

She kept her checkbook out. "But I took up your time."

A smile curved the corners of his mouth. "Call it catching up."

"I intend to pay for Cody's sessions," she insisted. Matthew had been a very rich man, even if there hadn't been a seven-figure life-insurance policy. "I didn't come here expecting charity."

"We'll discuss the fee schedule when and if the time comes," he qualified. "Rita can give you a copy. But today wasn't a session. It was a conversation. I don't charge for conversations."

She inclined her head, accepting the explanation for now. Maybe she was being too touchy. Ever since her world had been upended, she'd had trouble keeping her emotions in check. "Rita?"

He was about to refer to the woman as his secretary but paused, hunting for a more politically correct term. "The administrative assistant sitting out in the reception area."

She nodded. "The one who frowned at me because I came in without Cody."

That sounded like Rita. "Rita likes to run a tight ship. She takes care of us."

"Us?"

"The other psychologists here and me."

Laurel rose to her feet, as did he. For a moment, she looked as if she were going to breach the space between them and hug him, but then at the last moment apparently she changed her mind and merely extended her hand.

"Thank you again, Trent. This means a great deal to me."

"I'm not making any promises. About anything." He knew she thought he was going to start seeing the boy, but he hadn't committed to anything more than an initial visit. "We'll take it one step at a time," he told her.

Laurel nodded. It was enough for her.

Her perfume, the same scent she'd worn when they'd been together, lingered in the room long after she'd left.

Chapter Two

A few minutes later, Trent crossed the common area where Rita held court from the center of a round desk. Her position allowed her, at a moment's notice, to turn her chair three hundred and sixty degrees to train her hawklike gaze on any of the four psychologists.

Looking in his direction, the small, dark-haired woman, whose short, sleek hair was just a wee bit too black to be real, obviously expected to have questions thrown her way. Ready for him, she opened her mouth to speak, then closed it again without uttering a word. An almost imperceptible hiss escaped through the slight gap in her front teeth.

Trent walked right by her.

It wasn't Rita he wanted to talk to. Instead, he knocked on the door directly opposite his on the other side of the waiting area. Since the small red light, signifying a patient inside, wasn't on, Trent didn't wait for an invitation. He followed up his knock by opening the door.

Still holding on to the polished bronze doorknob, he stuck in his head and asked the room's single occupant, "Got a minute?"

Kate Marlowe stopped making notes and looked up. Laying down her pen, she smiled, then gestured for him to come in.

"For you? Always." As her stepson walked in and closed the door behind him, Kate pressed the intercom on her telephone. "Hold all my calls for a few minutes, Rita."

In response, there was a rather audible sigh on the other end of the line. "All right, if that's what you want."

Kate laughed softly. She was positive that somewhere someone had coined the word *crusty* to describe Rita. The woman rarely, if ever, smiled and no one knew how old she was. Kate had inherited her from the man whose practice she'd taken over years ago. According to him, Rita had come with the building. Kate had no reason to doubt him. The woman was resourceful, loyal and utterly opinionated. And despite prodding on Kate's part, completely devoid of a personal history. Kate felt a great deal of affection for her. It had something to do with her protective streak.

"Don't pretend that putting people on hold isn't one of your favorite pastimes, Rita. Don't forget, we go back a long way."

"If you say so, doctor," Rita murmured. The line went

dead. Kate expected nothing less. Rita wasn't given to wasting words.

Taking her finger off the intercom, Kate glanced up at Trent. She didn't need a degree in psychology to see that he was tense, that something was bothering him even though he tried to appear nonchalant.

Tall, with sandy-blond hair and sharp blue eyes, Trent had grown up into a handsome young man, just like his brothers.

Exactly like two of his brothers, she thought, suppressing a fond smile. Trent was one of triplets and to the untrained eye, each of them, Trent, Trevor and Travis, appeared to be carbon copies. It was only by paying strict attention that the subtle differences began to emerge. One's smile was brighter, another held his head a certain way when he was making a point, a third's eyes were just a wee bit bluer than his brothers' when he became impassioned about a subject.

What all three shared—along with their older brother, Mike—was a huge capacity for love and empathy. Although she had come into their young lives at a crucial point, she didn't pretend to take credit for the way they'd turned out. Their better traits had been there all along, she maintained. All she had done was to enable them to raise those traits to the surface.

She couldn't love Trent and his brothers any more than if they had been products of her own gene pool instead of Bryan and his first wife's. If pressed, in a moment of weakness she might have admitted to having a tiny, softer spot in her heart for Trent because he'd opted to follow her in her chosen profession.

"Does this have anything to do with Laurel?" she asked once Rita's voice had faded from the room and he still hadn't said anything.

Trent's eyes widened, and then he laughed. "You know." For some reason, he'd just assumed that Laurel had come and gone without anyone noticing—except for Rita, who made *everything* her business. "Why doesn't that surprise me?"

"I'm a mother," Kate replied simply. "Mothers are supposed to know everything." Her smile broadened. "You know that."

He could remember, as a boy, taking shelter in that smile. She made the hurt go away.

"You know," Trent said, some of the tension ebbing away from him as he made himself comfortable on the tan sofa, "when you first came to take care of us, I was pretty sure you had eyes in the back of your head." He flashed a grin. "Over the years, I became convinced of it."

"An extra set would have certainly helped, having the four of you to keep track of." There had been incidents with falling department-store mannequins and abruptly-halted escalators that she would just as soon put out of her mind. "But this time it was the eyes in the front of my head that made the connection. I saw Laurel leaving your office and heading toward the elevator."

Seeing the young woman again after all this time had caught her off guard. It brought back memories of how heartbroken Trent had been when the young woman had abruptly vanished from his life with just a terse note to mark her passage. He'd tried hard to pretend that everything was all right, but she had seen through him.

Instead of firing an array of questions at him, Kate waited for Trent to pick up the thread of the conversation. After all, he had sought her out and he would tell her why in his own time.

Kate didn't have long to wait.

She saw the tension return to his shoulders. "Laurel wants me to treat her son."

He was doing his best to sound removed, she thought. "Do you think that's wise?" she asked him gently.

Restless, Trent rose to his feet. "No."

Kate knew her sons very well. Reading between the lines wasn't hard. "But you're going to do it anyway."

A dry laugh escaped his lips, but the humor didn't reach his eyes. "Maybe you should give up psychology and become a clairvoyant."

Kate didn't believe in clairvoyants. She did, however, believe in instincts and being close enough to someone to almost "feel" his thoughts.

"My 'powers' only work with my family." She became serious, wanting him to talk it out as much as he could. "You wouldn't be in here if you were at peace with your decision, and it was fifty-fifty—telling her no or telling her yes." One slender shoulder beneath the powder-blue jacket lifted and fell in a careless shrug. "I've always been rather lucky at guessing."

Rising from her desk, she went to stand next to him. He

was close to a foot taller than she was, but he always felt she was the dominant force in the family. His father referred to her as the iron butterfly. The description fit.

Kate placed her hand on his arm. "Do you want to tell me about it?"

He shrugged, still feeling at sea about what had just transpired in his office. The surprise of seeing Laurel again after all this time had thrown him off. He assumed his stepmother was asking him about the case.

Trent shoved his hands into his pockets. "I don't know too many of the details at this point. According to Laurel, her six-year-old son, Cody, hasn't uttered a word in a year. Not since his father died in a car accident."

"He was there when it happened." It wasn't a question.

He looked at her only mildly surprised. "How did you know?"

It was strictly textbook so far. "The boy's behavior is a reaction to a trauma. At that age, it would most likely be a visual one." She paused a moment, thinking. "At least, that's the outer layer."

Trent wasn't sure he followed. "Outer layer?"

Kate nodded. "There has to be some other underlying cause for him to have withdrawn from the world, from the mother I'm assuming he had a decent relationship with until this occurred." The cadence at the end of the sentence told Trent that this was a question.

"I didn't ask, but knowing Laurel—" He stopped abruptly and smiled sheepishly, transforming into the boy he'd once been so many years ago. "I don't know Laurel," he amended, realizing he was making assumptions he had no basis to make. "At least, not the person she's become." Because the Laurel he'd known hadn't wanted the intimacy needed in a marriage, but this Laurel had married. Married, apparently, less than six months after leaving him.

"In my experience, most people don't change all that much," Kate commented.

He thought about Laurel, about the way she used to be. "She did."

"What makes you say that?"

"She got married," he replied simply. He realized that might need some explaining. "I asked her to marry me and she took off, saying she couldn't be in that kind of committed relationship with a man." He'd had his own commitment issues, but for Laurel, he was willing to try to work it out. Sadly, the feeling had not been mutual. He set his mouth hard. "Apparently, she got over that."

If Kate noted the sliver of hurt in his tone, she gave no indication. "Not necessarily." He eyed her sharply. "She could have dared herself to take this hurdle, or been shamed into it, made to feel less than a woman if she didn't commit. You don't know until you have all the facts."

It occurred to him that Laurel hadn't given him any details about her marriage, or even indicated how her husband's death had affected her. Her entire focus had been the boy.

"We didn't talk that long," he told his stepmother. "Besides—" he shrugged carelessly "—that's all water under the bridge."

Kate knew better. This nerve was very much alive and well. But for his sake, she made a light comment and pressed on.

"Very eloquently put, Dr. Marlowe." A smile played on Kate's lips and then she grew serious. "So, what are you going to do?"

He stared out the window for a moment before answering. Outside it was another perfect day in paradise. The sky was a brilliant shade of blue. As blue as Laurel's eyes, he caught himself thinking.

Taking a breath, he looked at Kate. "I said I'd see him tomorrow morning. I guess I'll know what I'll do after that."

"Sounds like a plan." She gave him an encouraging smile. She was proud of him, proud of the men all her sons had become. "Trust your instincts, Trent. You're a good psychologist and terrific with kids. Just because this boy is the son of someone you used to be very close to doesn't change any of that."

That was exactly what he was afraid of. Would his past feelings for Laurel cloud his perception or destroy his ability to assess the boy? He honestly didn't know—and his first priority was to the patient.

"Maybe you should see him," he suggested.

"I can do a consult, certainly," Kate agreed. But if Laurel had wanted someone else to see her son, she would have asked. "Laurel trusts you and the way she feels transmits itself to the boy. That's an important part of this healing process."

He sighed. "I know."

"Give it a shot, Trent," she encouraged. Her eyes met his. "I've never known you to turn away from a challenge."

"This is a boy, Mom," he pointed out, "not a challenge."

But she shook her head. "This is both," Kate corrected.

She was right. As usual. He tried to remember the last time she wasn't—and couldn't. "Don't you get tired of always being right?"

Kate pretended to think his question over. "No." And then she grinned. "When that starts happening, you'll be the first to know," she promised.

Moving around quickly, getting in her own way, Laurel placed her purse next to the front door, then doubled back to pick up the lightweight jacket she'd retrieved out of the closet for Cody. She hurried him into it. It felt as if she were dressing a mannequin.

This'll be over soon. Trent'll find a way to bring him around, she promised herself, trying to steady her trembling hands.

"You'll like him, Cody." She did her best to sound upbeat and hopeful, praying that *this* time something in her voice would get through to him. "He's someone I used to know before your dad. When I was in school." Moving around to face him, she zipped up his jacket. His arms hung limply at his sides. His eyes, unfocused, didn't see her. "The first time I met him, I guess I was just a little older than you. He's very nice."

All the words tumbling out of her mouth felt awkward on her tongue. That was because she felt awkward.

Awkward with her own son.

How had she come to this place? She and Cody had always had so much fun together. He'd been her saving grace when things had gotten so bad with Matt. And now, now she didn't even know him.

Laurel supposed that was what had finally driven her to seek out help from a field she would have never thought to tap. She'd never believed in psychiatry or its cousin, psychology. They were for neurotic people with too much time and money on their hands. But now she was rethinking *everything,* and she was desperate.

She felt estranged from her own son. Worse than that, she felt as if she were losing him, as if he were slipping away into some netherworld that only he occupied.

She looked down into his face. It was vacant, as if there were no one there. Laurel pressed her lips together, struggling against a wave of hopelessness.

These days, Cody didn't even look at her when she talked to him. He didn't disobey her, didn't throw tantrums, didn't show any emotion at all. It ripped her heart out that he behaved as if she weren't even in the room. She supposed it could have been worse. He did go where she told him to go, ate what she set in front of him and went to bed when she told him. But she missed him terribly. It was like having a windup toy, a clone of her son. He looked like Cody in every way except that there was no personality, no sign of the laughing, bright-eyed, intelligent boy he'd been a year ago.

More than anything else in the world, she wanted him back.

Laurel went to the door and picked up her purse, sliding

it onto her shoulder. For the thousandth time, she cursed her cowardliness for not standing her ground that day. The last day of Matt's life. She didn't believe in omens, but she'd had an eerie feeling all morning, a feeling that something would go wrong. Some unnamed instinct had told her to keep Cody close, to either keep him home or go with him. She'd chalked it up to her general uneasiness at the time. Matt had dropped his bomb on her only the night before.

Divorce was an ugly word and it had sent tremors through her world.

When she'd tried to tell Matt about her premonition, for lack of a better word, he'd called her manipulative and vetoed both of her ideas. Cody wasn't staying home with her and she wasn't going with them. He was breaking Cody in on the life of a time-shared child.

Nerves had danced through her like lightning bolts during an electrical storm as she'd watched them drive away.

Watched Matt drive away for the last time.

"He's very nice," she repeated to Cody.

Tears came to her eyes. They seemed to come so easily these days. She'd sworn to herself that she wouldn't allow Cody to see her cry, but since he hardly ever looked at her, it seemed like a needless vow.

"Oh, Cody, come out, please come out," she pleaded. "Talk to me. Say something. *Anything.*"

Her entreaty didn't seem to penetrate the invisible wall that surrounded the boy.

With a sigh, she pulled herself together. "It's time to go, Cody."

As if she'd turned on a switch, the boy walked toward the door. She opened it and he walked outside in measured steps.

"Maybe Trent will have better luck," she murmured under her breath, silently adding, *Please, God, let him have better luck. I don't know how much more of this I can take.*

"Trent, this is my son, Cody."

Framed in the doorway of his office the way she had been yesterday, Laurel stood behind the boy. She rested her hands lightly on her son's shoulders, as if she were afraid that withdrawing them would make Cody disappear.

Trent immediately rose to his feet. He'd been in the office a full forty-five minutes before this first appointment of his day, preparing. Preparing what, he wasn't certain.

He'd never felt anxious about meeting a new patient before. Oh, there'd always been that minor shot of adrenaline to begin with, but that was to be expected. He'd never been anxious before. First sessions were about ground rules, about getting to know the face that was turned to the world. Even children had their secrets and it was his job to unlock them so that his small, troubled patients could go on to have happy, well-adjusted lives.

But how did you prepare for a child who wouldn't talk? Who perhaps *couldn't* talk despite not having anything physically wrong with him. He knew firsthand that the bars a mind could impose were stronger than any steel found in a prison cell.

As he watched Cody now, it startled him how much the boy resembled Laurel. Neatly dressed, Cody's silken blond hair was a bit longer than stylish. A testimony to the free spirit that Laurel had so desperately strived to be, Trent recalled. If Cody's hair had been longer, he would have been the spitting image of Laurel at eight.

The Laurel, he thought, who had captured his heart the first moment he'd seen her. Was eight too young to fall in love? He would have said an emphatic yes if he hadn't been there himself.

Approaching the boy, Trent held out his hand. "Hello, Cody, my name's Trent," he said in his warmest voice.

Trent didn't believe in standing on formalities or drawing a sharp line in the sand to separate children from adults. Every adult had a child within him and every child harbored the makings of the adult he was to be. Trent focused on uniting them rather than keeping them apart.

Cody stared past his shoulder as if he hadn't spoken. As if there were no one else in the room but him.

Trent dropped his hand to his side. It was at that moment that he stopped thinking about himself and about Laurel. All that mattered was the boy in the prison of his own making.

Chapter Three

It was time to get started. Trent shifted his eyes toward Laurel, who was about to sit down on the sofa.

"Laurel, would you mind taking a seat outside in the reception area?" Laurel stopped and eyed him quizzically. "Rita looks formidable, but we have it on good authority that she doesn't bite. At least, we've never seen her do it," he deadpanned.

He tried to use humor to ease her out of the room, but it didn't work. The concern on her face intensified.

She glanced toward Cody uncertainly. The boy remained oblivious.

"I can't stay?" It wasn't a question as much as a request.

Unless he specifically called for a group family session, he found that parents, however unwittingly, tended to interfere with their child's progress far more than they helped.

"It's usually better if patients don't feel someone is looking over their shoulder during a session." Trent lowered his voice. "They tend to open up more."

Distress entered her eyes. "But I'm his mother. I only want to help him." Realizing that her voice was close to cracking, Laurel stopped for a second to collect herself. Even so, there was a plea in her voice as she said to Trent, "I want to understand what's wrong."

He sympathized with her, he really did. But it was far too early to bend the rules. He needed to see what he was up against and how deeply entrenched Cody was in this silent world. For all he knew, the boy might be reacting to his mother. He needed time alone with the boy to assess a few things for himself.

Very gently, Trent took her arm and steered her toward the door.

The brief, almost sterile contact awoke distant memories of other times, happier times. Times when he had believed that the world was at their feet. Before he'd learned differently.

But that was then and this was now, Trent reminded himself. And she had sought him out in a professional capacity. As a licensed clinical psychologist, he had both an oath and a duty to live up to and they both revolved around doing the best for his patient. In this case, her son.

"So do I," he told Laurel quietly. Out of the corner of his eye, he watched Cody. Usually, when an adult's voice dropped, a child did his or her best to listen more closely. Cody didn't appear to have even noticed that anyone was speaking. "And so does Cody." He saw hope flicker in her eyes. "Progress in cases like this is very slow and I need to do everything possible to make Cody feel more comfortable."

Whatever that might be, he added silently.

"He's not comfortable with me?" It was one thing to feel it, another to hear it said out loud. She felt as if her heart were being squeezed in half.

"He's not comfortable with himself," Trent told her.

The revelation took her aback. She searched for something to cling to, however small.

"You've had cases like this?" she asked, recalling what he'd just said.

If Trent had had cases like this, then maybe he really could cure Cody. A shaft of hope shot through her. She *knew* she'd been right in coming to him, even though she'd been hesitant at first, afraid of the ghosts that might crop up between them. The ghosts of things that hadn't been and the things that had. She felt far too vulnerable to cross that terrain again.

And far too guilty.

"Not personally, no," Trent admitted. He hadn't been practicing long enough to have encountered a wide sampling of the afflictions that affected a child's behavior. He saw Laurel's face fall. "But I read a lot," he said, offering her an encouraging smile.

His hand still on her arm, he opened the door and looked out into the reception area. Rita's small brown eyes darted in their direction the second the door was opened. It was, he thought, as if her eyes were magnetically predisposed toward movement, no matter how quietly executed.

Gently, he ushered Laurel out of the room. "Rita, would you please get Mrs. Greer some coffee?"

Laurel shook her head, declining. "No, I'm not thirsty." At the moment, with her stomach knotting, coffee would only make her nauseous.

"Good," Rita pronounced. Her tiny, marblelike eyes slid up and down like the needle on a scale. With a minute jerk of her head, she indicated the leather chair against the wall. "You can take a seat over there." It was more a royal command than a suggestion.

Laurel nodded, then looked at Trent. A shaky breath preceded her words. "If you need me—"

He gave her his most reassuring look, even as he tried *not* to recognize that her mere presence slowly unraveled something within him, something that had been neatly stowed almost seven years ago. He'd thought it would never see the light of day again.

Wrong.

"I know where to find you," he responded, his mouth curved in a kind smile.

Walking back into his office, he noted that Cody still stood stiffly. Trent closed the door and focused on his challenge.

"You can sit down if you like, Cody," he said in an easy, affable tone. "The sofa's pretty comfortable if you'd like to try that out."

Rather than sit down on the sofa, Cody sank down on

the floor right in front of it, his back against the leather, his legs crossed before him as if he were assuming a basic yoga position.

Or preparing to play a video game seated in front of a television set, Trent realized. He made a mental note to explore a few video games that he might substitute later for the ones that dominated Cody's attention.

If he continued with the case.

"Floor's not bad, either," Trent allowed, never skipping a beat as the boy sank down. "Mind if I join you?" he asked.

He'd found that keeping a desk between himself and his small patients only served to delineate territory, making him out to be an unapproachable father figure. He liked being close to his patients physically to help breach the mental chasm that could exist—as it obviously did in this case.

Cody made no indication that he had heard the question. His expression remained immobile as he stared off into space.

The boy's line of vision seemed to be the middle shelves of his bookcase, the ones that contained children's books he sometimes found useful, but Trent decided not to comment on that at this time.

"I'll take that as a yes," Trent said, lowering himself down beside the boy, careful to leave Cody enough personal space to not feel threatened. He looked around and smiled. "Looks like a pretty big office from down here," he commented amiably, then glanced down where he was sitting. "Also looks like the rug might stand to have a cleaning."

Neither comment, meant to begin to create a sense of

camaraderie, drew any reaction from Cody. It was as if his voice, his presence, were as invisible to him as the air.

"You know," Trent continued in the same tone, "your mom's pretty worried about you." He noticed just the slightest tensing of Cody's shoulders when he mentioned Laurel. It heartened him that there might be a crack, however minute, in the six-year-old's armor plating.

Trent turned his attention to the elephant in the room, watching Cody intently beneath hooded lids. "She told me that you lost your father a year ago."

Still not acknowledging Trent's presence, Cody abruptly rose to his feet and walked over to the large window. Tilting his head down ever so slightly, he appeared to look down at the parking lot four stories below.

For the moment, Trent remained where he was, talking to the boy's back. "It must have been hard, losing him at such a young age. You know, I lost my mom when I was five. Leaves a big hole in your heart, something like that," he continued conversationally. "It also makes you afraid. Afraid that everyone's going to leave you, even though they say they won't."

Knowing Laurel, he was certain she had tried to do everything she could to reassure her son that he was loved and that she would always be there for him. She'd mentioned her mother, so there was more family than just Laurel. Her late husband could have come from a large, close-knit family and there might be a lot of people in Cody's world, but that didn't change the fact that he might still feel alone, still feel isolated. Fear didn't take things like logic into account.

Trent considered the most likely causes behind Cody's silence. It could be as simple as what had plagued him all those years ago when he'd lost his mother, except that Cody had taken it to the *n*th degree, locking down rather than dealing with the fear on a daily, lucid basis.

Not that he had, either, at first.

"And sometimes," Trent went on as if this were a two-way conversation instead of only the sound of his own voice echoing within the room, "you wind up being afraid of being afraid. You know, the big wave of fear is gone and you think maybe everything'll be okay, but you're afraid that maybe those feelings will come back. I know that's how I felt for a really long time."

Trent shifted on the floor, trying to get comfortable. He envied the flexibility of the very young.

"The funny thing was, my brothers felt the exact same way I did. Except that I didn't know because we didn't talk about it. I thought there was something wrong with me because I felt like that."

Trent crossed his fingers and hoped that the boy was listening.

"That's the real scary part, not realizing that there are other people who feel just the way you do. That you're not alone," he emphasized, and then he sighed. "I guess if I'd talked about my feelings to my brothers, I would have found that out and I wouldn't have been so unhappy. It took my stepmom to make me realize that I wasn't alone and that what I was feeling—lost, scared—was okay." He ventured out a little further. "I felt angry, too."

As he spoke, Trent continued to watch Cody's back for some infinitesimal indication that he'd heard him, some change in posture to signify that his words had struck a chord with the boy. That he was getting through, however distantly, to Cody.

When he mentioned anger as another reaction he'd experienced, Trent noted that Cody's shoulders stiffened just the tiniest bit.

Anger. Of course.

Why hadn't he assumed that to begin with? he upbraided himself. Laurel said that Cody engaged in video games that exclusively involved cars. If he focused on crashing them, that was an act of hostility.

Trent wondered how much anger smoldered beneath Cody's subdued surface. A measure of anger was a healthy response. Too much indicated a problem up ahead.

Something they needed to prepare for.

He continued talking in an easy, conversational cadence, trying to ever so lightly touch the nerve, to elicit more of a response, however veiled it might be. These things couldn't be pushed, but children were resilient. The sooner they could peel away the layers, the better Cody's chances were of going back to lead a normal life, free of whatever angst held him prisoner.

"I was angry at my mother for being gone, angry at the plane for crashing. Angry at my father for letting her go by herself, although there wasn't anything he could have done if he'd gone with her. He certainly couldn't have stopped the plane crash, even though I thought of him as kind of a superhero. I probably would have wound up being an orphan," he confessed. "But that's the problem with hurting, Cody. You don't always think logically. You just want the hurt to stop.

"You just want your dad to come back even though you know he can't." He'd deliberately switched the focus from himself to the boy, watching to see if it had any effect.

He stopped talking and held his breath as silence slipped in.

Surprised by the silence, or perhaps by the fact that the hot feelings inside of him had a name, Cody turned from the window and actually looked at Trent for a moment before dropping his gaze to the floor again.

Yes! Score one for the home team, Trent thought, elated.

Given Cody's demeanor, he'd estimated that it might take at least several sessions before the boy had this kind of reaction. In this branch of treatment, at times it was two steps forward, one step back, but for the moment, Trent savored what he had.

The boy was reachable, that was all that counted. It was just going to take a huge amount of patience.

Laurel glanced uneasily toward the closed door.

What were they doing in there? Had Trent managed to crack the wall around Cody? Even a little? Had her son said a word, made a sound? Something? Anything at all. Oh God, she hoped so.

The waiting was killing her.

Cody had been talking since he was ten months old. Sentences had begun coming not all that long after that. His pediatrician had told her that Cody was "gifted." Matt had called him a little chatterbox. Cody could fill the hours with nonstop talk. So much so there had been times she longed for silence just to be able to hear herself think.

Remembering, she flushed with guilt. She would give anything to hear him talk again. These days, she tried to fill the void by keeping on a television set. And when that was off, radio chased away the quiet. *Anything* to keep the oppressive silence at bay.

Laurel looked away from the door. Staring at it wouldn't make it open. There was a magazine on her lap. It had been open to the same page now for the last thirty minutes, ever since she'd reached for it and pretended to thumb through the pages for the first two minutes. The articles hadn't kept her attention and although her eyes had skimmed the page, not a single word had managed to penetrate.

Just as her words didn't seem to penetrate Cody, she thought ruefully.

Trent had to fix him, he *had* to.

She had her strengths and she had learned to endure a great many things, but seeing Cody like this wasn't one of them. The idea of her baby being trapped in this silent world for the rest of his life simply devastated her. It was all she could do not to fall to pieces at the mere suggestion that Cody would never get better.

Fidgeting, Laurel caught herself looking at the closed

door to Trent's office for what had to be the tenth time. It was a struggle not to let another sigh escape her lips.

She could feel the receptionist—Rita, was it?—looking at her.

Clearing her throat, her fingers absently moving the magazine pages back and forth between them, Laurel asked, "Has he been in practice long? Trent, um, Dr. Marlowe, I mean."

Rita took her time in responding. "Depends on your definition of *long*."

Laurel shrugged helplessly. She had no definition for *long*. She was only trying to make conversation to pass the time.

"Five years?" she finally said.

Rita moved her head from side to side. The short, black bob moved with her. Her eyes remained on the woman sitting so stiffly in the chair.

"Not that long. The other Dr. Marlowe has been in practice fifteen years," Rita told her. "Ever since she took it over from Dr. Riemann."

"Oh," was all Laurel said. The single word throbbed with preoccupation. Her mind raced with thoughts she was afraid to examine.

Rita began to rise from her desk, as if to see to a task. But then she shrugged and sat down again. "Five minutes," she said to the boy's mother.

Laurel's head jerked up. The receptionist had said something to her but she hadn't heard the words. "Excuse me?"

"You've got five minutes," Rita told her, enunciating each word as if she were talking to someone who had to read lips. "The session, it's fifty minutes," she explained. "You've got five more minutes to wait."

"Oh." The light dawned on her. Laurel forced a smile to her lips and inclined her head. "Thank you."

Rita said crisply, "It's customary to pay up front and then I'll give you the paperwork so that you can mail it in to your insurance company."

She didn't work. Matt hadn't wanted her to. Hadn't even wanted her to finish college, saying, at the time, she was "fine" the way she was. She realized later it was all meant to control her. Matt liked being in control of everything and everyone.

Shaking her head, she informed Rita, "There is no insurance company."

Squaring her shoulders, Rita informed her with feeling, "Then payment is definitely up front."

"We can make arrangements later," Trent told Rita as he walked out of his office, catching the tail end of the conversation.

Laurel popped to her feet as if she'd been sitting on a spring that catapulted her into an upright position. Startled, she pressed her hand to her chest as she swung around. "I didn't hear you."

"It's the carpet," he told her with a smile. "It muffles everything."

Laurel wasn't listening. She was looking at her son, aware that she'd been holding her breath.

"Leave Mrs. Greer's account to me," Trent told Rita.

It was obvious that this wasn't what the older woman

wanted to hear. Accounts and the billing were her domain. She frowned. “I take care of *all* the accounts, Dr. Marlowe.”

After several years, Trent had gotten used to Rita and her rather unique ways. At bottom, as Kate had pointed out more than once, the woman was a huge asset. He smiled at Rita. “Change is a good thing, Rita. You should learn to embrace it.”

Rita made a noise under her breath and went to get the copy paper.

“I can pay my bills, Trent,” Laurel informed him. And then she glanced at her son. Cody seemed just as withdrawn into his own world as ever. She knew it was too soon for a miracle to take hold, but that was what made them miracles. Facing Trent, her heart rate sped up just a little as she asked, “Well?”

“Not yet, but he will be,” Trent promised.

Chapter Four

Kelsey Marlowe didn't hear the knock on her door at first. Lost in her studies—why did it seem like there was *always* another big exam looming on the horizon?—she didn't become aware of the noise until a louder rap echoed against the wood, startling her.

The next second, the door opened and one of the triplets peered in. Even after all these years, a first glance always made her mentally scramble for a clue to which one it was.

Kelsey realized that it was Trent invading her space about half a beat before he spoke.

"Hi, Kel." He flashed a smile that was just this side of serious. "Got a minute?"

Uncrossing her legs, she said the first thing that came to her mind. "No."

Open textbooks, not to mention her laptop, littered her comforter. Two of the books slid onto the floor with a grating thud. The pages she had them opened to disappeared.

Stress and surprise ate away at Kelsey's usual good humor. "You know, there's a reason the door was closed." She exhaled a huff that was filled with frustrated anger. "Does the word *privacy* mean anything to you? I could have been naked."

If she had been, he knew the door would have been not just closed but locked. Trent walked into the sunny bedroom. The only one of them still living at home, Kelsey had gotten the room with the best exposure. It used to be his.

He grinned. "This from the kid Mom had to chase after because you liked running around the house naked."

Embarrassment threatened to change the color of her cheeks. Kelsey struggled to suppress it, not wanting to give Trent the satisfaction.

"I was two," she reminded him indignantly. Were her brothers ever going to forget about that? She'd gone on to get straight As in every subject in school. Why couldn't they refer to that instead of the period of her life when her social values and awareness hadn't kicked in yet?

Trent shrugged good-naturedly. "Still, all the body parts were there." His grin widened. "And I've got a great memory."

She frowned at him as she tossed her head, her long, straight blond hair flying over her shoulder. "Obviously all long term. Your short-term memory appears to be shot."

Curious, he bent down to pick up the textbook that had dropped on the side of the bed closest to the door and handed it to Kelsey. “What did I forget?”

She took the book from him. The answer was right there in his hand and he still missed it. Men were hopeless, she thought. “That I have midterms coming up. I’m on quarters, not semesters, remember?” There was no sign of anything dawning on her brother. It figured. “I mentioned it at dinner Sunday. A dinner I had to move things around in order to make,” she added with a touch of exasperation.

“You mention a lot of things,” he pointed out in self-defense. He’d never come across anyone who could talk as much as his sister. Someday, he fully expected the muscles in her jaw to lock up. “Most of the time, you do practically all the talking at the table.” Again, he shrugged. “I filter things out sometimes.”

Sometimes? Kelsey laughed dryly. “How about all the time?”

That wasn’t true, but there was no point in going around and around about it. “I didn’t come here to spar with you.”

Sighing, Kelsey dragged her hand through a torrent of long blond hair.

“Okay, why did you come?” she asked.

Trent took a seat on the edge of her bed. “I need a favor.”

She didn’t have time for this, she thought. As it was, she was only averaging about four hours of sleep a night. “And I need to learn how to do without sleep,” she lamented.

Sympathy emerged. He wasn’t all that removed from his college years. “That bad?” he asked.

She sighed before gesturing at the books on her bed. "Pretty much."

Trent got up, careful not to send anything else sliding. "Sorry I bothered you."

He was leaving? Without telling her what he wanted? Her sense of curiosity wouldn't allow it. "Hey, wait, where are you going?"

Trent stopped short of the doorway, looking at her over his shoulder. "The favor I need requires time and you obviously don't have any."

Kelsey caught her lower lip between her teeth. Damn him. Trent knew how to push her buttons.

She gestured for him to come back in. If that hadn't worked, she would have hopped off the bed and physically pulled him back. But she didn't have to. Trent returned under his own steam. "You came here to talk to me, you might as well talk."

Trying not to smile, Trent sat down on the edge of the bed again. This time the action created an undercurrent and another textbook slid off on the other side.

Watching it, Kelsey struggled with a momentary desire to send *all* the textbooks to the floor with one grand, angry sweep of her arm.

Trent's eyes held hers. Hers were a darker shade than his. His expression was completely serious. This was important and he was making a judgment call. "I need you to tutor someone for me."

Something stirred within her. This was the first time any of her brothers had asked her to do something involving the vocation she'd finally decided on. Trent was treating her as an equal, as an adult. She'd finally lived to see the day.

For as long as she could remember—after she'd given up, at seven, the notion of being the first queen of the United States, she'd wanted to become a teacher. Not just a teacher but one who worked with children who had special needs, specifically the families who couldn't afford special schools to help their children catch up with their peers.

"What's wrong with him?" she asked, then made a guess, choosing the most common problem. "Dyslexia?"

If only, Trent thought.

He began by giving his sister the positive side first. "Cody's really very bright." During an extended lunch, he'd gone to Cody's school to talk to his teachers. The ones who had taught him before the accident. Once Trent had made the teachers comfortable with his reasons for asking—and his credentials—he had gotten what he was after. Confirmation.

If anything, Laurel had downplayed the boy's abilities. Before his father's death, Cody'd had read at a fourth-grade level while still in the first grade and, according to his teacher, Mrs. Bayon, he had been articulate, outgoing and happy.

"But his father died a year ago and Cody withdrew from everyone," Trent told her. "His grades are all down. He's on the way to failing everything but sandbox one-o-one." He knew that would elicit pity from Kelsey and, judging from the look in her eyes, he was right.

"Why?" she asked. "Lots of kids lose a parent early in life. They don't all respond like this. You didn't. Trevor, Travis and Mike didn't. Dad told me," she added when he looked at her, mildly curious. "What makes Cody different?"

"Well, for one thing, he was with his father when he was killed in a car accident."

"Oh." Incredibly empathetic, Kelsey instantly thought how she would have felt if she'd been in that situation. Her heart twisted and went out to the boy she hadn't even met. That made up her mind for her. "When would you want me to get started?"

He had known he could count on her. "As soon as possible." And then a stab of guilt made him ask, "Can you?"

She shrugged. "I could eke out a few hours on Saturday and Sunday," she speculated. "Maybe an hour or two during the week."

He didn't want to put her out, but he also knew in his gut that she was the right one for the job. "Anything would be great, really."

He sounded so enthused. A red light went off in her head. This was, after all, her brother, the one who used to plant crickets in her bed. Was this some kind of setup?

At the very least, she needed reasons. "Why come to me?"

Trent's answer was simple. "Because you're good at it."

She thought that herself. But there was a flaw in his answer. "You've never seen me work with kids."

He smiled at her. He didn't blame her for being leery.

He'd done his share of teasing when it came to Kelsey. They all had. But Kelsey could hold her own with the best of them, which was why he knew he had been right to come to her.

"Call it instinct," he answered. "I know when you do something, you don't do it by half measures. And you've had experience, student teaching. You don't get the kind of grades you do by slacking off." Kate had told him all the effort Kelsey put into her projects with the children. Only a completely dedicated person would go those extra miles.

Kelsey looked at him for a long moment, stunned. "That is probably the nicest thing you've ever said to me."

He grinned, nodding. "Yeah, it probably is," Trent agreed. "Don't let it go to your head. By the way, I don't expect you to do this for free. I'm going to pay you."

"You couldn't afford me," she informed him. She didn't want his money—she wanted his soul, she thought, swallowing a chuckle. "I'll figure out some way for you to pay me back."

"Should I be afraid?" Trent deadpanned.

Kelsey paused for a moment, pretending to think about it. And then she nodded. "Yeah."

He had to get going. Rising from the bed, he kissed the top of her head. "You're the best."

"About time you noticed that," she sniffed, pretending that the comment didn't get to her.

"I'll get back to you and fill you in on the details," he promised, beginning to leave. And then he remembered that he'd left out something. "Oh, one more thing. Cody doesn't talk."

Her eyes widened in surprise. "Doesn't talk?" she echoed in surprise.

Trent took a couple of steps back toward the bed. "Not a word since the accident." He watched Kelsey for a moment. Was she going to back out? He didn't think so, but there was always that chance.

And then she sighed as she shook her head. "You do like giving me a challenge, don't you?"

He let go of the breath he'd been holding. "Nothing I don't think you're up to."

Her mouth dropped open for a beat, and then she rallied. "Damn, two compliments in one session and me without my recorder."

His hand on the door, Trent winked at her. "Next time."

"Yeah, like there's going to be one," she murmured, getting back to her studies.

Trent closed the door behind him, grinning.

It was early evening and Laurel almost ignored the doorbell when it rang. She wasn't expecting anyone and she didn't like unexpected visits these days. But the doorbell rang again and she had a feeling that whoever was on the other side wasn't about to go away until she sent them on that route.

One glance through the peephole made her quickly pull the door open.

Laurel stared wide-eyed at the man on her doorstep.

What was he doing here? How did he know where she lived? And then she remembered that she'd had to fill out all those forms at his office.

Idiot. She upbraided herself for being so naive.

She didn't bother trying to force a smile to her lips. "Did I forget something?"

He knew he should have called first. But he'd been afraid that she might come up with an excuse, or ask him outright not to come and there were things he needed to ask, things that had to be cleared up before he could go forward with Cody's treatment.

"I just wanted to talk to you a little more about Cody." He was standing on her doorstep and she wasn't making a move. A smile quirked his mouth. "Mind if I come in?"

The question brought her around. She'd been using her body like a roadblock, unconsciously positioning it between the door and the doorjamb.

Laurel pressed her lips together. What was the matter with her? She was the one who'd come to him. This was for Cody, not her. Everything was for Cody. She no longer figured into anything, she silently told herself, except as Cody's mother.

"Sorry." Taking a step back, she opened the door wider. "Do you want to see him?" she offered, shutting the door again after Trent was inside. "Cody's upstairs in his room."

It wasn't Cody who could give him answers to his basic questions, it was her. He needed the answers in order to treat the boy. "No, I came to see you," Trent told her.

"Oh?" The single word seemed to shimmer with her barely hidden nervousness.

She was afraid he was going to ask her about them, about why she'd walked out. As much as he wanted to, that inquiry had no place here. "I need to ask you questions. I'm asking them as his doctor, not as…"

For a moment, his voice drifted away as he searched for a neutral word.

He needn't have bothered. She raised her eyes to his, valiantly struggling for a touch of humor. "My old boyfriend?"

"Something like that," he allowed, then admitted, "except more P.C."

In her opinion, people hid their true feelings far too much as it was. Feelings needed to be properly channeled and displayed, not buried under rhetoric because a crowd of people might misunderstand and possibly take offense.

"I don't have much use for P.C.," she murmured, her fingers knotting together. "Look, Trent, maybe I owe you an explanation—"

It was the elephant in the room. A huge elephant that took up almost all the space, sucked out almost all the air. But that was personal and he was here in a different capacity. He was here as Cody's therapist and until such time as Laurel told him that his services were no longer necessary, Cody was his first—and only—priority here, both professionally and otherwise.

Even if in the dead of night sometimes, when sleeplessness would stalk him, he'd lie awake and wonder why she had decided to leave him.

He did his best to sound removed as well as believable. "You don't owe me anything, Laurel. That's all in the past and we've moved on. I'm here because of Cody. If I'm going to help him, I need as much input, as much information, as possible," Trent told her matter-of-factly.

Well, if he wasn't here because of unresolved issues from the past, why was he here? "Rita had me fill out a health history for Cody while I waited." It was a comprehensive form that demanded a complete medical history, leaving nothing out.

Trent shook his head. That wasn't the aspect that had his attention. "That's not what I meant," he told her. "You said you had Cody completely checked out physically."

Again, she nodded. "By several doctors. Two pediatricians and a neurologist," she reminded him, in case he'd forgotten what she'd told him the other day. "And a G.P."

"No brain tumors or aneurysms, right?"

The very question sent a shiver down her spine. She remembered sitting in the hospital, scared to death as Cody had lain, so small and pale, on the table, disappearing into the MRI machine. She'd never prayed so hard in her life.

"No," she breathed. "None."

"Then something psychological is responsible for the problem," he elaborated. That was, after all, why she had come to him in the first place, to find the underlying cause for Cody's muteness. "Our daily lives, consciously and subconsciously, trigger responses, and not everyone reacts the same way to the same stimuli. For instance, an abused child—"

Red lights went off in her head instantly. Trent had been the only one, besides her mother, with whom she had shared that dark section of her past. "Cody wasn't abused," she protested heatedly.

"I'm not saying he was," he told her. It was still a very sensitive spot with her, he thought, like a button that couldn't be pushed. "But an abused child can go one of two ways. He can grow up to be an abuser, or he can be a loving parent in an effort to never make the mistakes his own father or mother made with him." He looked at her pointedly. "There are a lot of contributing factors that go into making us who and what we are."

She was looking at him the way she used to, Trent thought for a fleeting moment. That unguarded look, because of what she'd shared with him, that had always made him want to protect her at all costs.

He struggled to bank down that feeling. The best thing he could do for her right now was to reach her son. That was the *only* thing he had to focus on, the only thing he needed to think about.

She wouldn't allow him to approach the other subject, no matter how much she needed him to or he wanted to help her. He'd supposedly made his peace with that.

Surprise.

Trent pushed on as if nothing had happened. "So picture this as a giant jigsaw puzzle," he suggested. "In order to put this together, I'm going to need all the pieces."

She took a deep breath. It made sense. She had to stop being so sensitive and just be grateful he was willing to help.

"All right." She gestured toward the kitchen. "Why don't you come into the kitchen and I'll make us some coffee?"

He followed half a step behind her, taking in his surroundings. Highly polished marble floors passed beneath walls devoid of color, decorated with paintings he had a feeling were originals, not copies. Expensive originals. It didn't quite look like a place where someone lived, only visited on their way to somewhere else. To home.

"Nice house," he commented politely.

Rather than agree or thank him for the compliment, Laurel looked around as if she hadn't seen it earlier. She shrugged and said, "Big house."

"You don't like it?" he asked. Then why was she staying? It seemed like a logical question, but he kept it to himself.

"This was Matt's house," she told him. "I moved in after we were married." She'd wanted a home that they had chosen together, but Matt had told her this was far better. Nothing needed to be done. And so, she had left no mark on it.

Why would you marry him and not me, Laurel? "So you never felt as if this was really your home?"

A protest rose to her lips, but then she shook her head. There was no point in pretending. He was right. This wasn't home, not really. Not even after all these years.

"No." And then she smiled. "You're good."

Trent easily deflected the compliment. "That was pretty much a no-brainer."

The kitchen, off to one side, was the kind that most gourmet cooks only dreamed about owning. A professional range was located beside a stainless steel industrial-size refrigerator.

Laurel noted the way Trent looked around. "Matt liked to do a lot of entertaining here," she explained, then added, "Clients."

His interest was already aroused. "What did Matt do?"

"He owned several companies," she answered, then realized how vague that sounded. But Matt had been vague whenever she'd asked him about his work. "To be honest, I never could pin him down to specifics. He'd give me a lot of double-talk when I asked." She opened the refrigerator and took out a container of coffee, placing it on the granite counter. "But there was always a reason for him to be on the road." She paused, her eyes filling with tears. "That was what was so bad about what happened. He was finally trying to bond with Cody when…" Her voice trailed off.

And then she rallied, squaring her shoulders, pulling herself together before Trent's eyes.

The coffeepot made a guttural noise, announcing that it was done.

About to open the refrigerator again, Laurel stopped and looked at him over her shoulder. "You still don't take cream or sugar, or has that changed?"

He smiled and shook his head. "That hasn't changed."

Laurel nodded. "Nice to know that some things haven't."

Chapter Five

"But he already has a tutor," Laurel protested. They were still in her kitchen, sitting at the table opposite each other like strangers. Or opponents. The small talk had gotten progressively smaller, until it had disappeared altogether like a wish that couldn't be granted.

In the face of her protest, he asked pointedly, "Is Cody making any progress?"

From what he'd gathered at their initial meeting, he already knew the answer to that—which was why he'd approached his sister about taking over.

Laurel frowned, looking down at the now cold coffee. The cam lights overhead shimmered along the liquid's surface, winking and blinking like fairies with a secret. She sighed. God, she was doing a lot of that lately, she thought.

"No. Not yet."

He measured his words slowly, watching her face for an answer. "How long do you want to wait before you decide to try someone else?"

She thought of the ads she'd read regarding the network of tutors she'd hired. They all promised results in the blink of an eye. There'd been more than several "blinks" already. It was hard to be patient when she felt the word *forever* whispering along the perimeter of her mind. What if Cody stayed like this for the rest of his life?

Laurel answered Trent's question with a question. "And this tutor is good?" she asked.

"Yes. I can personally vouch for her."

Her.

Was he talking about someone he was involved with? Laurel wondered. And why in God's name would that make her discontent? Did she think his life was just going to stand still? That Trent would now be exactly as she'd left him? Her life had gone on. There was no reason in the world to believe that his hadn't.

And yet, that was what she *had* believed. Damn, maybe she should have found a psychologist for herself, as well as her son.

You can't go home again.

"Then, you know this tutor well?" she heard herself asking, words scraping along a dry throat.

"As well as anyone can know anyone," Trent told her and then grinned, remembering his exchange with Kelsey just before he had come to see Laurel. "I've even seen her stark naked."

The second the words were out, he realized what they had to sound like to Laurel. That he was romantically involved with this tutor. Was that a glimmer of sadness in her eyes? Did it matter to her what he'd done with his life since she'd left it? Most likely not. It was just a reflection of wishful thinking on his part, he told himself.

"She was two at the time," he explained quickly, punctuating his statement with a laugh, "and I'm talking about my sister."

"Kelsey?"

Okay, either his imagination was working overtime, or he heard relief in her voice. Or maybe just incredulity.

The last time Laurel had seen Kelsey, she had been a rather obnoxious fourteen-year-old, always popping up where she wasn't wanted and fussing loudly when she was asked to leave. He could remember one time when he could have literally wrung her neck. She had ruined what could have been a very romantic scenario.

"She's not the same bratty fourteen-year-old she was back then. There's been a huge change in the last seven years—for the better," he emphasized. "We actually like her now."

Seven years. It had been that long, hadn't it? Seven years could be an eternity for some. Especially if those seven years had been spent living in an ivory tower, feeling cut off and isolated from the world.

Matt had kept her like that, away from her friends until they'd moved on. It had taken her a while to realize how controlling he was, not just of his empire, but of her, as well. He had felt he owned her the way he owned the companies he helmed. He had kept the latter until he had lost interest. He had been set to do the same with her—until death had stopped him.

"Kelsey's getting her degree in special education," Trent said. Laurel wondered if he'd detected her thoughts drifting away for a moment. "And she's very passionate about her work. I think she can help Cody catch up, especially being as gifted as he is."

The description caught her by surprise. "Are you going by what I told you?"

But even as she asked, she played back his words in her head. Trent had said *is,* not *if.* That meant he was sure. After just one session? That didn't seem possible, since Cody had kept his silence during the whole fifty minutes. Trent would have told her if Cody had said a single word.

"You'd be slightly biased," he allowed with a smile. "No, I talked to his teacher, the one he had before the accident," he qualified before she could ask. "Beth Bayon had nothing but praise for him. She thought it was awful that he'd shut himself up like that."

He was about to tell her that weekends worked best for Kelsey, but a loud crash from somewhere within the house interrupted him.

As if that were some sort of a signal, Laurel was on her feet instantly.

"Cody."

It was the only word that broke from her lips as she ran

out of the kitchen. She raced up the stairs before Trent could catch up to her. He hurried behind her and together they entered Cody's room.

He'd never seen a child's room that was so large. Its walls were lined with books, toys, games and everything imaginable that a boy could want. It struck Trent that there was nothing left to desire. Every wish that a six-year-old could utter appeared to have already been granted.

The video-game console that was the current rage and last Christmas's "must-have" gift was lying upside down on the floor where Cody had obviously sent it sailing in a fit of anger. Its connections to the wide-screen flat-panel TV were severed, a casualty of the same surge of fury.

Cody stood in the center of the bedroom, his face red with rage and an impotence that prevented him from channeling his feelings properly.

"Cody," Laurel cried again, falling to her knees beside the boy. She threw her arms around him and tried to hug him to her, offering comfort the only way she knew how. Avoiding eye contact, Cody shrugged out of her grasp, swung ninety degrees to his right and kicked the console.

Before he could kick it again, Trent picked up the console, holding it out of range. "Has he done this before?" he asked when Laurel looked at him in surprise.

"No." A desperation thickened the walls of her throat, threatening to close off her windpipe. She could feel it filling up with tears. She struggled against a wave of hopelessness. *It was going to get better. It had to.* "No," she repeated, "this is something new." Again she put her arms around Cody. This time she held on as tightly as she could. Cody couldn't shrug her off. "Cody, please, stop," she pleaded. "I love you."

"He knows that," Trent told her gently. He looked down at the console he held. Despite Cody's angry punt and its unscheduled trip through the air to the floor, it looked remarkably none the worse for wear. He raised his eyes to Laurel's. "This shouldn't be in his room."

Freeing her son of her embrace, Laurel rose to her feet. "But that's the only thing that seems to hold his attention. Besides the cars." She glanced over to a pile of toy cars in various stages of destruction. He used to love those cars, she thought sadly.

"Fine," Trent acknowledged. "But this—" he raised the console slightly "—should be in the family room. *He* should be in the family room," he added, nodding at Cody, "not sequestered in his room."

Sensitive, she bristled. Trent made it sound as if she'd sent Cody to his room as punishment—or because she didn't want to see him. "I don't send him there, he wants to be there."

Trent watched her for a long moment. "You're the mother, Laurel," he said, pointing out the obvious. "Where do you want him to be? Out of sight, or where you can see him?"

He knew the answer to that, she thought angrily. Why was he even bothering to ask? Did he think she was some addle-brained woman for whom motherhood was a burden? "Where I can see him, of course."

He didn't rise to the bait of her angry voice but went on

talking quietly, stating what she already knew in her heart to be true.

"Then it's up to you to put him there. If this is what he likes to do—" he indicated the console with the game still loaded inside it "—then it should stay in the family room."

"Matt hooked the console up for him." It was an advanced model. She remembered how excited Cody had been. And how Matt had looked at her in the midst of it all as if to say, *See, what do you have that could possibly compete with what I can give him?* "I don't know how to attach it to the set in the family room," she confessed.

"Neither do I," Trent told her honestly.

He looked down at the boy, who had calmed down remarkably, to the point that it hardly seemed possible that he'd displayed such a flare of anger only minutes before. The boy had a great deal of pent-up anger inside. They needed to find a proper way to channel it so that it could be purged without harm.

"How about you, Cody?" he asked. "Do you know how to hook the console up to the television set?"

Laurel looked at him as if he were delusional. "He's only six," she protested.

"You'd be surprised what they can do these days," Trent told her, never taking his eyes off the boy.

Ordinarily, he'd ask to see the manual. Handy enough himself, he'd hooked up his Blu-ray player recently and sincerely doubted if this video-game console were all that different. But he thought that this might be a way to get the boy to come around, and he wanted to see what Cody would do.

After a beat, still not making eye contact or even acknowledging Trent's presence, Cody put his hands on the video console and drew it away from him. Instead of leaving his room, he turned around as if he intended to reconnect the device to the television.

Trent quickly stepped in front of the boy, blocking access to the set.

"Sorry, champ. New rules. It can't go there. If you want to play video games, you're going to have to hook the set up downstairs—so that your mom can watch the games with you if she wants."

Cody's eyes darted toward his mother, but it happened so quickly that it might have just been a trick of the lighting.

A small sigh escaped the boy's lips. But rather than surrender the set, this time he headed out the door into the hall.

Trent saw Laurel looking at him, a half-hopeful expression on her face. Her silence begged for a confirmation. Rather than say anything, Trent gestured for her to follow Cody. Trent fell into step behind her.

By the time they got to the family room, Cody was already plugging in the console and attaching the connecting wires that he'd ripped out upstairs.

Trent crossed over to the boy as he watched what Cody was doing. "Great job, Cody."

Praise came easily to his tongue because of the way he'd been brought up. Kate had never doled out praise sparingly. Rather than criticize, she had always focused on the positive, on the things her children had done that pleased her rather than on the things they had neglected to do. It didn't take much time for there to be far more of the former and a great deal less of the latter.

Trent followed her example in his practice. Good mental health began with a good self-image. He needed to reinforce the one Cody had of himself.

"It would have taken me a lot longer to do that," he told the boy. "And only if your mom knew where the instruction manual is."

Cody still didn't look at him, but Trent noticed that the boy's slim shoulders appeared to be a little straighter now, rather than slumped the way they had been just a few minutes earlier in his bedroom.

"You want to show me how to play the game?" Trent asked. "My sister likes to play video games to relax, but I never got into the habit. Maybe I should," he continued amiably. Trent paused to look at the disc label that peeked out of the console. Letters streaking across a lightning bolt. *"Blaze of Glory,"* he read. "Is that your favorite?"

Rather than answer, Cody switched on the set, then the console and planted himself, cross-legged, before the flat-panel, a control pad in his hand. He took a position off to one side, to leave room for Trent if he wound up joining him.

Nothing happened by accident. Trent took it as a good sign.

"Is there another control pad?" Trent asked. Cody made no response, his fingers dancing along the left and right sides of the control pad. Trent looked at Laurel. "Do you know if…?"

"Matt bought two," she remembered. "He was going to play with Cody, I guess, but like a lot of other things, he never managed to get around to it. I don't know where it is," she apologized.

"That's okay." He glanced over his shoulder. Cody's attention was on the screen and the cars whizzing by at top speed.

For now, he'd accomplished enough, Trent thought. He'd gotten the boy to come out of his room and interact with him, however distantly. He felt more than satisfied.

Taking Laurel's arm, he guided her to the far side of the room to talk to her in private. "I can get one for next time."

She looked at him in surprise. He intended to come back? Here? "Next time?"

Trent nodded. Turning so that he could keep an eye on the boy, he told Laurel, "I think it might do him more good if I work with him in familiar surroundings. He'll feel less threatened and that way he might let down his guard a little sooner."

Oh, if only, Laurel thought. "So, you'll be coming here to see Cody, instead of my going to your office with him?" It was a question that really didn't need an answer, except that she needed to hear it. Needed to come to terms with it. She wasn't sure how she felt about Trent being here. It felt too personal, might unlock too many things that weren't adequately buried.

"Yes." Trent studied her face. There had been a time when

he had known it better than his own. When he could almost read her thoughts. Until he couldn't. "Is that a problem?"

What was wrong with her? This wasn't about her, about them or even about mistakes that couldn't be undone. This was about helping Cody. *Only* about helping Cody.

She squared her shoulders before answering. "No," she said, shaking her head. "No, why should it be?"

"You tell me," he said. "Do you feel like I'm encroaching on your territory?"

Laurel crossed her arms over her chest. He could always read her like a book, she thought. He'd guessed without any effort at all. The truth of it was, they were already getting too close, too personal, and he hadn't even begun the bulk of his work with Cody. Who knew how long that would take? To have Trent here was an invasion of her space. It made her feel—what? She thought, searching for the right word.

Vulnerable? Nervous? Excited?

Matt hadn't been gone a year. How could she feel this kind of antsy anticipation when her husband hadn't been dead even for twelve months?

Things had not been good between her and Matt for a long time, she reminded herself. And he hadn't been the man she'd thought he was. Still, she couldn't shake a feeling of guilt, as if by having Trent here she were somehow dishonoring Matt's memory.

He was going to take Cody from me. Remember that. Why should I feel guilty about anything when it comes to Matt?

"Laurel? Laurel, are you all right?" Trent asked, concerned.

He was gazing at her with uncertainty. *He probably thinks I've become a space case.* Pulling herself together, she blocked any further thoughts as she flashed him a reassuring smile.

"I'm fine," she told him with feeling. "And I have no problem with you coming here. Why should I?" she bluffed. "The only thing I want is to have Cody back the way he used to be, before the accident. And whatever it takes to get him there is more than fine with me. So, yes, you can come here and, yes, you can bring Kelsey if you think that she can help him more than the tutor that I got for him." Laurel paused and looked at him pointedly. When she spoke again, her voice was low, as if she were imparting a secret meant just for the two of them. "I trust you, Trent, I always have."

He struggled to ignore the effect her voice had on him. Maybe she wasn't aware that she was lying, he thought. But he was. If she'd trusted him, *really* trusted him, then Cody would be their son, not just hers, because they would never have broken up.

But she hadn't trusted him, and they had broken up. Even so, there was no use in his pointing that out to her. Laurel would only deny it. The past was the past and it needed to remain that way, especially if he intended to do the boy some good—which he did.

"Good," Trent finally said, glancing in Cody's direction. The boy was completely focused on the game, his body moving with the cars as they hugged the road, first left, then right, then left again.

Satisfied that the boy had calmed down and was engrossed in the racing game, crashing cars when the opportunity arose, Trent nodded toward the kitchen. "I believe that we've got two cups of rather cold coffee still waiting for us."

She'd forgotten all about that. Forgotten, too, what his smile could do to her. Tie her stomach up in knots. "I can make fresh coffee," she volunteered.

He shook his head. "No need. Most of the coffee I drink is cold by the time I get around to it. I still have questions," he said conversationally.

"I might have answers," she countered, trying her best to sound cheerful.

The operative word here, Trent thought, was *might.*

Chapter Six

Trent had just settled in to catch up on some paperwork when his phone rang. He noted the caller ID a second before he put the phone to his ear and said, "Hello."

"If you want me to tutor Cody today, you're going to have to swing by the house to pick me up."

No social amenity had preceded his sister's statement. He'd wondered why Kelsey would be calling him at this hour of the morning. It was nine and she was supposed to be en route to Laurel's house to work with Cody, the way she'd been doing for several weeks now. Kelsey had been very faithful about giving the boy some of her spare time on weekends. When he'd thanked her, she'd shrugged it off, saying that working with Cody was good practice for her. She'd confided that, despite his silence, she was making some headway and that she really liked the somber six-year-old.

A Marlowe through and through, Kelsey admitted that she saw getting Cody to talk as a challenge she was fully determined to meet. She'd gone as far as offering to make a little side bet on who Cody would speak to first. Because it added a little color to the situation for her, Trent had finally agreed.

It took him a second to process her impatient statement. Kelsey hated being late these days. It was a by-product of going to college. Prior to that, time had been an arbitrary factor in her life.

Trent switched the phone to his other hand as he pushed papers back into a manila file. He had a feeling he wouldn't be getting to them this morning. "Something wrong?"

He heard a rustling noise in the background. "Only if you call a dead car battery something wrong. Mom and Dad are out and the car refuses to start. I could get a jump-start from the guy next door," she told him, "but then what do I do once I get to Cody's house?" She answered her own question. "Get another jump-start?"

Because she left the last sentence hanging in the air, Cody realized she expected him to jump in and volunteer his services.

The notes he'd brought home to transcribe would just have to wait. He rose to his feet.

"Okay, hang on. I'll be there in ten minutes," he promised. "Lights permitting."

Some of the tension left her voice as she told him, "I'll be the one standing next to the dead car."

"Thanks," he deadpanned, getting his keys off the bureau. "Otherwise I would have asked you to hold on to a red rose so I could recognize you."

"Wiseass," she murmured under her breath.

He laughed, terminating the call and shoving the phone into his pocket. "Right back at you, Kel."

Laurel was more than a little surprised when she saw Kelsey *and* Trent coming up the winding front walk. A moment ago, she'd glanced out her window to see if Kelsey was pulling into the driveway. It had been ten minutes into the young girl's time with Cody, and Kelsey, just like her brother, was *never* late.

Ever since the accident, the word *late* held particular uneasiness for her. Because *late* could very easily mean *never.*

Throwing open the front door, Laurel banked down the urge to meet them halfway. Instead, she stood in the doorway.

Kelsey seemed a little agitated.

"Something wrong?" Laurel asked.

Kelsey let out an annoyed breath before answering. "My car died," she said, crossing the threshold into the house. "Trent volunteered to drive me over."

"The kind of volunteering they do in the army," Trent elaborated. Laurel appeared uncomfortable, he noted. As if his unexpected arrival had thrown her. He thought they'd gotten past that. Obviously not. "I can wait in the car if you like," he offered.

"No, no, don't be silly." She looked toward Kelsey. "Cody's upstairs in his room."

Kelsey was already at the stairs. "I figured," she responded cheerfully.

Alone with Trent, Laurel collected herself. She wiped the palms of her hands on her jeans. "I can make you some fresh coffee," she proposed.

Trent shook his head. "I don't want to interrupt anything. Go back to whatever you were doing," he urged, adding, "Just pretend that I'm not here."

She laughed softly under her breath as she turned on her heel and made her way to the kitchen. "That's like standing in the presence of the aurora borealis, pretending that the sky is the same black color it always is at that time of night."

"Okay," he allowed, walking into the kitchen behind her. "Don't pretend I'm not here." He slid onto one of the two stools that were usually tucked under the counter. "Talk to me instead."

Why did that elicit such a nervous flutter in the pit of her stomach? "About?" She did her best to sound almost disinterested.

"Anything you want," Trent told her glibly. And then his voice dropped. He continued watching her. "Or don't want."

"Trying to get me to bare my soul again?" she asked. He'd already attempted that twice and she'd avoided his questions both times. She wasn't comfortable talking about her life after she and Trent had broken up.

She moved about her kitchen like a butterfly that had no idea where to land for more than a single heartbeat.

Yes, I want you to bare your soul to me, he thought. But out loud, he said, “Not really.”

Because she was moving about so nervously, he slid off the stool and leaned his hip against the long, blue-black granite counter. He studied her for a moment. She looked like a woman on the verge of a breakdown.

And why not? Look what she had to deal with. Her husband had been killed in a freak accident and her son was in a prison of his own making.

“Are you talking to anyone?” he asked her softly. Laurel’s head jerked up. The coffee ready, she pushed a cup in his direction, taking hers in both of her hands. He couldn’t read the expression on her face. He proceeded on as if she were merely puzzled and not indignant or annoyed. “About how you feel about everything that’s happened,” he elaborated.

Laurel’s eyes narrowed. “I don’t need a psychiatrist,” she told him tersely. Not everything could be solved by sitting around and talking. There’d be no absolution for her no matter how long she talked.

“I didn’t say you did,” he answered mildly. Still holding her cup, Laurel walked back out to the family room and he followed. “But everyone needs someone to talk to.” He sincerely felt she needed to open up—and was fairly certain that she hadn’t. “They don’t necessarily need a professional license on the wall to be able to listen.”

Laurel placed her cup on the coffee table but remained standing, as if it would allow her to deflect his words more successfully.

"I've made my peace with everything."

His eyes held hers. "Have you? Every time I ask you about your marriage, you shut down or change the subject." So far, he had tried several times, broaching the subject from different directions.

How much of it was for Cody's sake and how much of it was for your own? he silently challenged himself. *She hurt you. Get over it.*

Laurel swung around, glaring at him. "Because it doesn't have anything to do with Cody's problem." And then she paused, not quite as sure as she had been a moment ago. A little of the fire left her eyes as she asked, "Does it?"

He sincerely believed it did. "We are a product of everything," Trent explained. "Not just genes, not just environment, but everything. We take things in and put our own spin on them, our own stamp that makes our reaction unique to us." And then, to get his point across, he gave her an example. "Two kids can be teased exactly the same way in school. One becomes an overachiever, bent on becoming a success to show his long-ago tormentors that he's better than they are, and the other becomes a serial killer, dealing with his feelings of inadequacy in a decidedly different way."

His examples unsettled her. Her eyes widened as she asked, "Are you saying that…?" Laurel couldn't bring herself to finish her sentence.

She didn't have to. Trent cut her off before she could complete the painful—and completely inaccurate—connection.

"I'm saying that if you and your husband fought or there was an undercurrent of trouble in the marriage, it might be affecting how Cody responds to you now."

Laurel shook her head. "Cody wouldn't have known," she protested. "Matt and I were careful not to let him hear us when we were arguing." She deliberately made it sound as if the discord were two-sided. But it was Matt who had raised his voice, Matt who had threatened. Matt who had made her feel so inadequate.

"You'd be surprised what kids pick up on and hear."

The thought of Cody hearing what Matt had said to her, the names he'd called her, caused a shiver to race down her spine. She couldn't bear the idea.

"Cody was five at the time," she reminded him. At five, the world was still small, still manageable. Friends, play, school, just a few ingredients. She realized that she'd left out home. "All he cared about was cartoons."

That was far too simplistic, Trent thought. She was deliberately clinging to that in order to deceive herself. He was right, there *had* been problems in her marriage. Apparently big ones.

"Cody was—and is—exceptionally bright. Your own words," he reminded her. "If he gave no indication that he sensed that you and your husband weren't getting along, he was trying to protect you. Or hoping that if he didn't acknowledge it, whatever was wrong would go away and you and Matt would be happy again."

She clung to her stand for dear life. "Cody's bright, but you're giving him far too much credit here."

Trent fell silent for a moment. It wasn't his habit to interject his personal life into his professional life. But this situation was rather unique. Laurel had been in his personal life, had once represented a very large part of it. And surrendering this piece of information was relevant. It just meant opening up a place that he wanted to keep untouched.

Still, this was to help her understand why he was asking her about her marriage—not as the man she'd left but as Cody's therapist. He braced himself before he spoke. There was no way to distance himself from what had once been. Just as he really couldn't distance himself from Laurel, couldn't think of her as just another patient's mother.

"Shortly before my mother was killed in a plane crash," he began, "I heard my parents arguing. It seemed that he wanted a family—us—and even though she'd given in, she felt trapped being a mother, especially since there were so many of us and we weren't exactly the most docile kids.

"She told my father she wanted to feel free again." The past vividly shimmered before him. "I don't know," he said honestly. "If she'd lived, they probably would have gotten a divorce eventually. But at that point, Dad was desperate. He encouraged her to take a short vacation—a break from us and from him—to see if she still felt trapped."

His mouth curved sadly. He remembered pressing his small body against the wall so that they wouldn't see him, listening and feeling strangely hollow inside, as if someone had emptied out his stomach. "It might have given her a chance to miss us."

He took a breath before continuing, doing his best to sound clinical—and failing miserably.

"That was why she was on that plane. She turned out to be the only fatality." A great many people had been hurt, he recalled, reading the article he'd found online years later, but Jill Marlowe had been the only one to die. "I blamed my father for 'chasing' her away. I blamed myself and my brothers for not being 'good enough' to make her want to be with us. In my own way, I guess I was pretty messed up and I coped with it by acting out." That had been perhaps the blackest period of his life—except the day he'd discovered that Laurel had all but disappeared into thin air.

"My brothers and I drove away three or four nannies in pretty short order before Kate came into our lives and had the wisdom and the patience," he underlined, "to deal with us.

"My point here is that I was five when my mother died and all this was going on in my head. I didn't realize it until I was older. And my behavior wasn't exactly unusual." He looked at her pointedly. Listening, uncomfortable with what he was saying to her, she sank down beside him on the sofa. "Cody probably heard, or maybe even sensed, that things were not good between you and Matt. Kids are just short adults, Laurel. They pick up on vibes as well as words."

Finished, he let his words sink in as he listened for the sound of his sister approaching. But Kelsey was giving Cody a longer session than she'd anticipated. There was time for more questions. If Laurel was up to it.

He picked up his cup and took a sip of coffee before quietly asking her, "Why were things not good between you and Matt?"

She shrugged. Where did she start?

"Why's the sky blue, Mommy?" And then she flushed. "Sorry, that was flippant." To her surprise, Trent laughed softly. Laurel blinked. Had she missed something? "What?"

"I didn't know you could be flippant. You've changed since..." To his credit, he managed to retain the smile on his lips, even if it had abruptly left his soul.

"Since," she echoed. There was no reason to go over their past history together. She knew she was to blame for what had happened. And she had paid dearly at the hands of another man. How often had she lain awake late at night, fervently wishing that she could go back in time. That she hadn't allowed her demons to make her walk away—no, *run* away from Trent.

With Trent beside her, she might have been able to deal with what had wound up sending her into Matt's arms. What had made her marry him.

"Yes, I have changed," she agreed. The changes should have been for the better, but she knew that some of them weren't. "Grow or die, right? Except that with Matt, there was no room for growth," she heard herself saying.

It was almost as if the words were rising to her lips of their own volition, tired of remaining in the dark, tired of existing in silence. She tried to backtrack, to save Matt's reputation because he was Cody's father. And because she looked like a fool for staying with the man she'd discovered beneath the polished veneer.

"Matt was the big, dynamic knight in shining armor who swept me off my feet. He was the type who, if he wanted to have Italian food, would have his pilot gas up the jet and fly to Rome for the evening. That was pretty impressive in the beginning." She remembered being initially awestruck by him. And stunned that out of a world full of women, he'd chosen her.

That was before she knew that the choice wasn't permanent. Or exclusive.

"What happened?" Trent asked.

"I got jet lag," she quipped. Her voice lowered, becoming more serious. "And Matt got bored." It was easier to say that than to admit the real truth. And, in a way, it was true. Matt had gotten bored. Because she couldn't be the woman he had wanted her to be. "I should have realized that a man who juggles half a dozen companies isn't the kind who can be tied down for long."

"I take it there were other women."

There was no point in trying to keep up the charade, especially if it got in the way of helping Cody.

"Yes, there were. Legions. I asked him to stop. He said he would. He didn't. So I threatened to leave him." Her mouth twisted in a humorless smile. "And he said 'fine.' But then he said that he was going to keep custody of Cody." That had been her Achilles' heel. Cody. "That kept me in my place for a long time—how could I fight someone as powerful as Matt Greer?

"But then my complicity with his lifestyle wasn't good enough for Matt. He'd gotten bored controlling my life and wanted to move on. He 'told' me that we were getting a divorce just before he left with Cody that day. And he also said that if I contested the divorce in any way—the terms, custody, anything—he'd make me sorry I was ever born." Laurel pressed her lips together. Remembering left such a bitter taste in her mouth. "My last words to him were 'I hate you.'" She looked at Trent. "And then he was dead."

"And you feel guilty?" He could hear it in her voice. The thought almost left him speechless.

"Yes." She shook her head, knowing she was being stupid. "No." But there were ambivalent feelings knocking around in her. She sighed, raising her eyes heavenward. "I don't know." And then she laughed at herself. When had life gotten so complicated, so out of control? She used to know herself so much better than she did now. "I can't even make up my mind about that."

"There are a lot of contributing factors at play here. It's not cut-and-dried."

His words almost gave her hope. Almost. But this was Trent. Trent, who she had treated badly. Trent, who she should have married when he'd asked her. By rights, he shouldn't want to have anything to do with her. Instead, he was trying to help her. Help her son. "*Why* are you being so understanding?"

He shrugged good-naturedly. "Nature of my job, I guess."

"But I left you."

Intellectually, he knew why. It was just that emotionally it had hurt like hell. "You were scared."

What kind of a man forgave like that? Men like that existed on the screen, in the conclusion of romantic comedies. They didn't walk the earth. Everyone had thought she was the luckiest woman in the world when she'd "caught" Matt because he was so fantastic—but he hadn't been.

"I still left you," she insisted. "Badly, as I remember. And then I turned around and married Matt less than six months after that." She was talking faster now, reviewing all the things he should have held against her. "Matt talked me out of finishing college." How could she have been so stupid? "God, my mother was so angry about that. Angry that I gave up everything for Matt." There had been more to it than that. More to her mother's anger about the union, but he didn't need to know that. It was hard enough to live with as it was.

Trent recalled that he had always liked Laurel's mother, a strong, independent woman. "She wasn't impressed by his wealth?"

"My mother was more impressed by you," Laurel confessed. "By your kindness." She paused and flushed ruefully. "I never told you that, did I?"

"No."

"My mother didn't exactly trust men, not after what my father… Not after my father," she ended, not wanting to go there. "But she did like you. Said you had wonderful eyes." And he did, she thought as she looked at them now. Warm, kind, beautiful eyes.

"Got to remember to put that on my résumé," Trent quipped.

They were sitting close now, closer than he'd intended, and tension seemed to shimmer between them. The kind of tension that crackled and flashed until it was given what it demanded.

The pull that had been there ever since he'd first seen her standing in the doorway of his office. Suddenly it became a force that couldn't be ignored.

Leaning forward, Trent lightly skimmed his knuckles along the hollow of her cheek. Something flared in her eyes.

Desire.

The same desire that now throbbed insistently in his veins. For one small moment in time, he wasn't Trent Marlowe, child psychologist. He was just Trent Marlowe, a college student who was hopelessly, head-over-heels in love with a young woman he had known since the fourth grade.

And had wanted since the beginning of time.

Tilting his head, Trent softly brushed his lips against hers, half expecting Laurel to pull back.

But she didn't. She remained exactly where she was. And kissed him back. Laurel parted her lips, offering up a silent invitation.

He slipped his arms around her, drew her closer and deepened the kiss as he felt a rush surge through his veins.

Chapter Seven

Laurel's head was spinning wildly.

It had been so long since she'd felt this way. Nearly a lifetime ago.

She'd forgotten how dizzying it was to kiss Trent. For a split second, the years abruptly melted away. They were college freshmen again with the whole world and its opportunities spread out in front of them.

Before the fear had all but crippled her and pulled her away. There was an incredible innocence back then, even though the chemistry between them had sizzled.

She had never slept with him. And he had been so achingly patient with her.

Oh God, she'd missed him. Missed feeling as if she

could soar with the eagles into a cloudless sky that was so clear, so blue, it almost hurt.

Because she so desperately needed it, Laurel surrendered herself to the sensation, to the moment, knowing that she would be safe. Though every system within her had gone on red alert, warring between desire and fear, she knew she was safe. Trent never pressed her to do anything she didn't want to do. She knew this wouldn't go beyond where it was right now.

Cody and Trent's sister were in the house and could, at any moment, come looking for them. She didn't really even want Cody to see her kissing another man.

But she couldn't stop.

The knowledge that they weren't alone gave her a sense of security, of having a safety net directly beneath her tightrope. It left her free to wrap her arms around Trent and her soul around the fiery longing that ran through every inch of her body.

One more second and he would be over the brink.

One more second of this and he was just going to pick Laurel up and carry her to her bedroom—wherever the hell that was in this mausoleum of a house.

He couldn't risk it. There was too much at stake. Not to mention that Kelsey was here. With great effort, Trent drew his lips away from Laurel's.

Shaken, they stared at one another, the silence throbbing, underscored by the sound of their mutual breathlessness.

Trent knew he should apologize, or at least make an attempt. But nothing came to him. Other than wanting to kiss her again. He didn't want to apologize for doing something that made him feel so alive.

Still, he had to do the right thing. There was a severe conflict here. Laurel might not be his patient, but her son was. He was pretty certain that sealing lips—and other body parts—with a patient's mother was frowned on by the ethics board.

But, rather than a halfhearted apology, a confession came to his lips. "I've been wanting to do that for a while now." He paused before forcing out the words, "I'm sorry."

Laurel needed to pull herself together, but she couldn't quite manage it. She wasn't sorry. Just scared. "Sorry that you did it, or sorry that you wanted to do it?"

The question took Trent by surprise and he paused for a moment, thinking. "I don't know," he finally said, honestly. "I'll have to get back to you on that."

"As long as you get back to me," she said in a whisper, intending the words more for herself than for him.

But he'd heard her. And he wanted to. Oh God, he wanted to. He wanted to get back to her in every sense of the word. To make love with her slowly, languidly, the way they never had before when they were together. He'd held himself in check back then, always stopping before crossing that last line.

Because that worthless excuse of humanity, her father, had abused her as a child, any kind of intimacy was difficult for Laurel. She had an inherent distrust of it—and ultimately of any man—even as they were drawn to each other.

Trent could understand that. And since he was dealing with issues of his own, he was patient with her. The trouble was, because of the way he felt about her, he'd ultimately worked out his issues but she hadn't worked out hers. He hadn't realized that until the day he'd proposed to her. She'd paled before his eyes and left him.

Ran from him.

It had hurt like hell.

He'd struggled to get it out of his system and eventually had. Or so he'd thought. He'd believed that after working so hard he was finally over her.

Until she'd turned up in his office with those soft doelike eyes of hers that could always burrow through his skin and hit him where he lived.

You just never get over some people, he thought now, as he tucked a stray hair behind Laurel's ear. His pulse continued to race.

Laurel had been his first love and that had left a huge imprint on his heart.

So had her leaving.

And now he was trying to deal with a new element. Trying to come to terms with the fact that she'd left him and married someone else less than six months later. Why had she trusted this corporate superstar and not him?

It didn't make sense.

From what he'd read on the Internet, the late Matt Greer hadn't been a bad-looking man and, yes, he'd been born with a platinum spoon in his mouth. Moreover, the fiercely competitive Greer had gone on to triple his worth by the time he'd reached his thirtieth birthday. But Laurel wasn't the type who cared about the size of a man's bank account.

Was she?

How well did he really know the woman who'd broken his heart? Trent didn't have an answer for that.

"You're staring at me," Laurel told him self-consciously. Did he think she was terrible? *Was* she terrible? Laurel didn't want to think so, but the truth was, she wasn't really sure *what* she was, other than utterly confused.

His eyes held hers. The moment stood still. "Just thinking."

"About?" She held her breath. If Trent thought she was awful, she had to hear it from him.

"What might have been. And wasn't."

Her heart stood still. And then ached. She owed him an explanation.

But how could she tell him that she'd married Matt, not because she'd wanted to, but because she'd had to? What she'd told him before about being swept off her feet had been a lie. The truth was, if she hadn't said yes, hadn't married Matt, her mother would have died.

Her mother knew why she'd married Matt—even if Matt, because of his enormous ego, hadn't realized why until later. And it was the one note of discord between them. Her mother had felt guilty about needing the funds and angry with herself for what she had reduced her daughter to. It was one of the reasons Grace Valentine never warmed to her son-in-law. Because in her eyes, her daughter had prostituted herself so that she could have triple-bypass surgery. Her mother's heart had gone on beating while hers had effectively stopped.

"Don't go there," Laurel entreated.

He laughed shortly. "Hard not to."

Laurel shook her head. "Won't change anything. There aren't any time machines around, Trent. And no way to change the past no matter how much we want to. There's just now."

"And the future." *Was* there a future with her? If he wanted it, was there?

She shook her head again. She was no longer the wide-eyed girl, clinging to tiny shreds of optimism and hoping that they would grow into a feeling, a philosophy. A way of life. If she had any hope left within her at all, it was all directed toward her son and, she prayed, his well-being.

"There's just now," she repeated.

"Laurel—"

Trent got no further. Whatever he was going to say was cut short because his sister chose that moment to walk into the room.

Perfect timing as always, Kel.

Collecting himself, he turned to look in Kelsey's direction.

"We're done for the day," Kelsey announced, then stopped short. She looked from her brother to Laurel. "Am I interrupting something?" she asked.

Not only bad timing, but not too subtle, either, Trent thought.

"No," he said, rising. "We were just killing time. Talking," he added for good form. And then he turned his attention to the reason the three of them were together in the first place. "How did it go with Cody?"

"Well," Kelsey said, nodding her head thoughtfully. Her lips curved into a bright, cheerful smile reminiscent of her mother's. "It went well. Cody is definitely catching up." Her eyes shifted toward Laurel. "A few more weeks and you won't need me."

Laurel looked at her, stunned. Afraid to hope. "That soon?"

Kelsey's smile widened. "He's a very bright boy," she told Laurel.

I knew that, Laurel thought. But the light had gone out of his eyes, out of his soul, and he had crawled into some dark cave where she couldn't reach him. Though a virtual stranger obviously had.

She had to know. "How are you getting through to him?"

"He hears me," she told Cody's mother. "He hears everyone," she added, glancing toward her brother. "I go over the lessons several times, show him shortcuts, give him ways to remember things."

Laurel wanted so much to believe her. But she'd been disappointed before. The special-education tutor before Kelsey had told Laurel after only three weeks that she didn't hold out too much hope.

"But how do you know that he's absorbing any of this?" His current first-grade teacher had said that talking to Cody was like pouring water on a highly waxed car. The words just beaded up, remaining on the surface without any indication that they had penetrated.

"I give him tests." Kelsey grinned. "And he aces them." His sister went on to explain her method and how Cody had worked up to answering full sheets of questions.

Trent saw pure joy flash in Laurel's eyes. She held her breath as she asked, "Really?"

Kelsey nodded her head, feeling rather proud of herself. "Really."

With a heartfelt sigh, Laurel threw her arms around Kelsey. She hugged the younger woman with enthusiasm. "Thank you."

"My pleasure." Still firmly gripped in Laurel's embrace, Kelsey turned her head toward her brother. Her eyes silently asked for help. "But now I've got to study for a test of my own."

As if suddenly realizing what she was doing, Laurel released her son's tutor and stepped back. But inside, she couldn't stop beaming. "Oh. Sorry. I didn't mean to keep you."

Through the heating vent, they heard the beginning jingle of the video game that Cody played daily.

"Since he did so well, I told him he could go play. I hope you don't mind," Kelsey said.

"No, no, that's fine," Laurel reassured her. Right now in her eyes Kelsey could do no wrong. "He needs a break." Smiling, Laurel blinked back tears, wiping away one that had escaped. "I don't know how to begin to thank you." Her eyes swept over Trent and his sister. "Both of you."

Cody still wasn't speaking, but she knew that Trent was

doing everything he could. Before coming to him, she'd started to lose hope, but now, with this, she was sure things would be all right. She just had to be patient, that was all.

"I'll leave that between you and Trent," Kelsey told her. The look on the woman's face was payment enough for now. "Now I *really* need to get back to studying. I'm afraid I can only give you about an hour tomorrow. I've got this massive test first thing in the morning on Monday."

"Of course, of course, I understand," Laurel said, walking them to the door.

They passed the family room. Laurel looked in. Cody's back was to the doorway and he appeared to be deeply engaged in his game. Maybe it was just her wishful thinking, but he didn't seem to be as intent on crashing vehicles as before. The car he was propelling was gliding back and forth around the track.

"See you tomorrow, Cody," Kelsey called out.

In a silent acknowledgment that he'd heard, the boy half cocked his head in the direction of her voice before turning his attention back to the screen.

Laurel and Trent exchanged looks, a single word hovering in both their minds. *Progress.* It was precious when it finally made its appearance.

"Thank you," Laurel said again just before they left the house.

The radiant look on her face would remain in his mind's eye for a long time, Trent thought as he quickly walked to his car.

He hit the security-release button on his key ring and

his Honda Accord squeaked twice. Kelsey lost no time in opening the passenger door and getting in.

"I didn't interrupt a meeting of the minds, did I?" she asked with a wide grin as she buckled up. When Trent's only response was a low grunt, Kelsey just continued as if he'd answered. "Although it looked more like a meeting of the lips to me."

So she *had* walked in before he and Laurel had drawn apart. Trent frowned, backtracking his way through streets lined with custom homes. "You're not supposed to spy on your betters, Kel."

"Hey, I was just coming in to report on the kid's progress." She laughed. "Not my fault you decided to play kissy-face with the lovely Laurel." And then she grew just a little more serious. "Correct me if I'm wrong, but isn't Laurel the one who stomped on your heart with her gorgeous, designer stilettos?"

He knew Kelsey's heart was in the right place, but that didn't change the fact that her nose definitely wasn't.

"That is none of your business."

"Mom would disagree with you, big brother. Much as it pains me to admit it, you're family and family is family's business."

She was parroting something that Kate had said more than once. Ordinarily, he would have agreed. Except that this was his life and that made it different.

"Sounds a lot better when Mom says it," he commented.

It began misting. He turned his windshield wipers on low and flipped on his headlights.

Kelsey didn't seem to take offense. "Everything sounds better when Mom says it. Doesn't make it any the less true," Kelsey informed him. He could feel her studying his profile. "Okay, so, what's the deal?"

"There is no deal," he told her. "Laurel's just an old friend and her son has an emotional problem. She came to me for help. That's what we're doing. We're helping out." He stomped on his brakes suddenly as an SUV darted out, cutting him off. He barely avoided hitting it.

Kelsey threw her hands up, bracing herself against the dashboard. "And my fee for my wonderful services is the truth."

Trent played dumb, pretending not to know what she was driving at. "So go ahead, talk."

"Truth from you," she emphasized. "I seem to remember that the two of you were together all the time when I was fourteen. And then you weren't."

He set his jaw hard, looking straight ahead. "That about sums it up."

Kelsey sighed. "I overheard Travis and Trevor talking right after she disappeared from the scene. They said that Laurel dumped you." She paused. "Did she?"

He thought of brushing her off, of telling her to butt out in no uncertain terms. But he knew she wasn't just being nosy. Kelsey cared. Just as he cared about Kelsey, despite teasing her at every opportunity. So he wrapped his answer up in a nutshell, telling her what he hadn't told anyone else. Because no one else had pressed this hard.

"I asked Laurel to marry me. She said no."

Kelsey looked at him, stunned. "Why?" And then she collected herself. "I mean, I'd turn you down, but she seemed pretty much into you as I recall."

That's what he had thought at the time. "Not enough to say yes." And then, because this was about Laurel, he grew protective. "She had a lot to deal with." Knowing that Kelsey was capable of going on and on, drilling deeper as she went, he turned the tables on her. "So, how's your love life?"

She shrugged, looking out the window. "Nonexistent, thanks to school and you."

"How about that guy you dragged by at Christmas?" The guy had been tall, lanky and had eaten as if there were no tomorrow. They'd all wondered where he put it all.

It took her a minute to remember who he was talking about. "Hayden's history."

There'd been others. Lots of others. Guys had always been attracted to Kelsey.

"How about the one with the earring? Roger, was it? I thought Dad was going to have heart failure when he got a look at him."

She blew out a breath. She didn't seem enthused about reviewing a cavalcade of her old boyfriends. "Okay, okay, point taken. You don't want me prying. You could have just said so instead of dragging out not-so-special people from my past."

"I did," he pointed out.

Yeah, he did, she remembered. Frowning, she asked, "Do you always have to be right?"

"No," he answered cheerfully, then slanted her a superior look he knew drove her crazy. "Only when I am."

Kelsey shook her head. "Good luck, Laurel," she murmured under her breath.

"What's that?" He tilted his head toward her to hear better.

"Nothing," she said quickly, then pointed in the distance in an effort to divert his attention. "Look, there's the house."

Trent grinned, satisfied he'd gotten his point across. "So it is."

Chapter Eight

The sharp, single *ding* sounded crisply in the kitchen, breaking into Laurel's thoughts. She realized that she was staring at the wall clock without really seeing where the thin black hands pointed.

When she heard the sound, her first reaction was to glance toward the front of the house. But it wasn't the doorbell she heard, just the oven.

Laurel sighed. She knew that old adage about a watched pot never boiling. Did that saying extrapolate to include doorbells as well? If you kept expecting them to, did they not ring? And when you stared at a timepiece, did time actually stand still? It certainly felt that way.

Rousing herself, Laurel crossed the short distance from the table to the oven. She took two oven mittens and slipped them on, then opened the oven door. Heat rushed out to greet her.

This was her third time checking on the cookies she'd prepared thirty-five minutes ago. Each of the other times, she'd had to push the timer back by five minutes because the cookies had still been too soft. The first time, they easily could have been consumed with a straw. But ten minutes beyond the recommended baking time the twelve giant "eating wheels," as Cody had called them when he was barely three, were finally solid enough to be done.

She removed the cookie sheet from the oven and placed it on top of the stove. She was far from being a gourmet cook, certainly not near enough to merit a kitchen like hers. But when Matt had been alive, there'd been a professional chef on staff, Barbara Hathaway, whose résumé read like a who's who of corporate America. Barbara had taken care of all the meals and had politely but firmly banned Laurel from the kitchen.

Once Matt was gone, she'd let Barbara go. There was no point in keeping the woman on, especially not at her salary. Cody hardly ate anything and her own tastes leaned more to sandwiches and pizza. If occasionally she had a craving for something more elaborate, she could make it herself or, better still, call one of the restaurants in the area and have them deliver.

Most of the time, she hardly made use of the kitchen beyond a simple breakfast or coffee. But today, because she kept watching the all-but-paralyzed clock and found herself needing a diversion, she'd thrown herself into making something she knew for a fact Cody used to love: peanut butter-chocolate chip cookies. She'd made them from scratch and silently crossed her fingers.

At least they look like cookies, she congratulated herself.

The scent of the warm cookies seemed to fill the kitchen. Laurel glanced over her shoulder toward the doorway. She was alone. She hadn't expected Cody to come running in, salivating like a bottomless, ever-hungry puppy. But she was still hoping that the cookies might just widen the ever-so-slight crack in the wall around himself.

At least she could hope.

Besides, searching for ingredients and making the cookies had helped to keep her hands, if not exactly her mind, busy. Trent was late and he hadn't called. It made her restless. She needed to do something.

In the background, Laurel heard the familiar jingle and intermittent crashes that were part and parcel of the one and only video game that still had a lock on Cody's attention. While the familiar was comforting—if nothing else, it meant that Cody was only a few rooms away—in this case, the crashing cars and screeching tires were getting under her skin, shredding her nerves one by one.

Where was he?

Abandoning the kitchen, Laurel made her way toward the front of the house and the large bay window that looked out onto the winding driveway. It wouldn't make Trent arrive any faster, but she couldn't help herself.

Laurel stopped short when she saw him.

Cody.

Her son stood so close to the window it seemed as if he'd wandered there on purpose. Unaware that she was nearby, the boy actually appeared to be looking out. Her heart leaped up in her chest. He was watching for Trent.

She pressed her lips together to keep from saying anything, sensing that if she made her presence known, he'd quickly bolt from the room.

Slipping back out of the room, Laurel smiled to herself. *You got through to him, Trent. You actually got through to him.*

A jumble of emotions raced through her. She felt like laughing and crying at the same time.

Had she really expected any less? This was why she'd come to Trent in the first place, risking the humiliating possibility of having him turn her down. In her heart she knew that Trent would succeed when everyone else failed. He would find a way into Cody's silence.

All right, the boy still didn't talk, but Trent had told her that Cody had made eye contact on more than one occasion. Moreover, he now appeared to respond when spoken to—nonverbally and through body language, Trent had qualified, but it *was* a response. And that was all that mattered.

Her heart swelled. She could almost feel it smiling. *Thank you, Trent.*

The moment she withdrew from the room, slipping back into the hallway, she heard the doorbell. At the same time, she also made out the rustling sound of what had to be retreat. Not wanting to be caught waiting, Cody was leaving the room.

Laurel quickly reentered just as her son was about to leave via the door on the far side of the room.

"Looks like he finally got here, Cody," she said cheerfully, as if they'd been engaged in a conversation all along. Out of the corner of her eye, she saw Cody stop and turn around.

Hurrying over to the entrance, she noted Trent's outline through the beveled glass on the upper half of the oversize door. Sunshine pushed its way through, scattering and forming rainbows on the marble beneath her feet.

"Sorry," Trent apologized the second she opened the door. "Traffic was a bear. There was a truck filled with tires overturned on the freeway. Bouncing rubber everywhere. Snarled up traffic so badly, it took forever just to get off and take the long way over here."

He seemed tired, she thought. Trent had set up the sessions with Cody for three days a week after his regular hours. Which meant that he'd already put in a full day treating patients before arriving here.

A shaft of guilt pierced her. This was taking advantage of their friendship. "Listen, if you feel you're too tired—"

He cut her off, shaking his head. "Nope, not me. I got a second wind. Besides, I brought a new video game for Cody." Taking it out of his jacket, he noted that he'd caught the boy's eye. Trent held up the game for Cody to see, then crossed over to him. "See, it's still got cars in it," he pointed out. "But before you can race them, you have to try to beat your opponent at building them up."

The idea behind the switch was simple. He wanted the

boy to focus his attention on being constructive rather than destructive.

Handing the video game to Cody, Trent stopped and sniffed the air. His eyebrows drew together as he turned to look at Laurel.

"Either you changed your perfume," he noted, "or somewhere in this house is a batch of freshly made peanut butter cookies."

Amused, Laurel laughed. They were several rooms away from the kitchen. "That's some nose you have there," she commented. "As a matter of fact, I just took a batch out of the oven."

Trent's eyes crinkled as he grinned. "I guess my timing's not so bad after all." He glanced over his shoulder at Cody. The boy was still looking at the game cover, as if absorbing the instructions. "Want some cookies, Cody, my man?"

Cody raised his eyes up to Trent's and, after a beat, actually nodded.

Laurel's mouth dropped open. That was a direct response. Cody was communicating with someone. "Trent," she began breathlessly before words deserted her and she became entirely speechless.

Trent gave her hand a little squeeze, silently telling her that he understood everything.

"If it's not too much trouble," Trent suggested, "maybe you could bring a sample of your cookies into the family room while Cody and I tackle this new game."

She just nodded, afraid that if she opened her mouth to say anything, her voice would crack.

* * *

When Laurel walked into the family room several minutes later, carrying a tray of cookies and milk, she received her second surprise.

Sitting before the TV set as usual, Trent and Cody were huddled over the back of the video box "reading" the instructions. Trent pointed out the words one at a time to Cody.

She nearly dropped the tray when she heard Cody utter a hissing sound when Trent pointed to, then carefully enunciated the word "should."

Steadying her hands, she murmured, "Sorry," when Trent looked her way.

Jumping to his feet, he took the tray from her. "Nothing to be sorry about," he told her easily. He set the tray on the floor beside the television set. "Cody and I are just going over the rules of the game." He saw joy mixed with confusion in her eyes. "Excuse me for a second, Cody," he said, addressing the boy the way he would an equal. "I need a minute with your mom."

Cody looked back down at the box in his hand.

Taking her arm, Trent guided her to the far side of the room. Her heart pounded in her throat. "He's talking?" she asked Trent in a hushed whisper laced with disbelief. A part of her had all but given up hope.

Trent shook his head. He didn't want her getting ahead of herself here. They were definitely making progress, but not by leaps and bounds.

"He's making sounds," he corrected her. "I'm teaching him how to express words through sounds first. A hiss for *s,* a growling noise for *r* and so on. It's a system used for children who suffer from selective mutism."

Laurel didn't know if she should be concerned or elated. She'd never heard of the affliction. "Is that what he has?"

"No," Trent was quick to assure her, "but the principle's the same. Kids with selective mutism can actually talk—and do—but they are so shy in certain circumstances that their jaws turn almost rigid on them. It's not a matter of refusing to talk, they physically can't. The way that's being treated is to get at the root of why they're uncomfortable. That's why I'm treating Cody at home instead of in the office, to make him more comfortable," he explained. "And while we're trying to achieve that zone of comfort, I'm trying to give him a way to attempt to express himself, by forcing sounds out."

Laurel stole a glance toward her son. She supposed that made sense. She'd taught Cody how to read by sounding out the words he didn't know.

"And that's how you'll get him to talk?" she asked hopefully.

He had to be honest with her, even though he would have liked her to go on being overjoyed.

"Not exactly." He saw her struggling with disappointment. "I still need to find out what's going on inside of him. *Something* is keeping Cody from talking. Now, whether his psyche is freezing him into place, or something else is going on, I don't know yet, but we're making progress, Laurel," he assured her. "It's just in baby steps."

Laurel held back a shaky breath. She knew he was doing the best that he could. "Baby steps," she echoed.

He had to get back to Cody. Trent gave her arm an encouraging little squeeze. "We'll get there," he promised, before turning back to his patient.

His words echoed in her head as she left the room. She clung to them.

"How about a field trip?"

She nearly bumped her head on the inside of the oven when she heard his voice behind her. Sitting back on her knees, Laurel brushed a strand of hair from her eyes with the back of her wrist.

As she turned around to look at Trent, her eyes narrowed slightly. Had she heard him correctly?

"A field trip?"

Trent nodded as he came closer. The idea had hit him just as he'd wound up his session with Cody. "To an amusement park. The three of us. Cody needs to keep being immersed in normal settings."

She was adorable, he thought, as unbidden memories reached out to him. Wearing jeans and an old shirt, her hair mussed, she looked very much the way she had when they had been together. He tried to ignore old feelings, not wanting them to get in the way of his judgment.

He cleared his throat. "I was thinking we'd go to Knott's Berry Farm. The park's relatively small and has a homier feel to it than some of the other parks. There's a petting zoo for kids his age."

She nodded. "I remember. I took Cody there for his fifth birthday." She started to get up. Trent took her by the arm and helped her to her feet. "You think he's ready for that?"

He wanted to experiment by placing the boy in a position where he could be part of a greater whole, yet feel that he had backup and support if he needed it, the crucial ingredients coming from his mother as well as from him.

"I do," Trent told her, "especially if he's been there before. Kids go to amusement parks all the time. Most natural thing in the world."

She and Trent had gone to that particular park a number of times the summer they'd graduated from high school. It had been one of their favorite places. They'd arrive when the doors first opened and stay the entire day, often closing down the park. She came to know every inch of the park by heart. More than that, she could remember every location in the park where he'd kissed her.

It seemed like a million years ago now. Or someone else's life.

As if reading her mind, Trent said, "You can invite someone else to come with us if you'd feel more comfortable." And then, because she didn't say anything, he added, "Your mom might want to come—or I can see if I can get mine to go with us."

"I don't need a crutch—"

"Didn't mean to imply that you did."

Laurel tossed her head. "I don't need a chaperone, either."

"I might want one," he told her with a wink.

Trent cupped her face with his hand and, for a second, she thought he was going to kiss her. Her heart stood still. Common sense told her she had to move back, to stop him, but the trouble was, she *wanted* him to kiss her. Wanted to be forced to recapture what had been.

To her surprise, rather than kiss her, Trent took a deep breath, as if sniffing the air around her. "Ah, essence of oven cleaner." And then he laughed as he released her face. "Same old Laurel," he commented. She looked at him, puzzled at his meaning. "You still clean when you're upset?"

It was her way of restoring order to things, making them clean. She shrugged carelessly. "This is a big house to take care of. I try to stay ahead of it whenever I can."

She hadn't given him a straight reply—which gave him his answer. But he pretended to go along with what she'd said. "You can't tell me there's not enough money for a housekeeper."

"There is, but I never liked strangers living in my house." She'd always been a private person. Maybe that was why she and Matt really hadn't been meant for each other. He had loved crowds, people hanging on his words, doing his bidding. Mundane details had never interested him. If anything, they irritated him. She remembered the look of annoyance on his face once when he had found her vacuuming. He had shut off the appliance and taken it away, saying he had "people" for that and he didn't want to see her doing chores again. His wife wasn't supposed to do housework. He hadn't said it out of kindness but because she'd unwittingly violated some rule of order in his world.

Trent filled in the blanks. "How many 'strangers' did you have living here when your husband was alive?"

"Three. The housekeeper, the cook and the chauffeur." *Four if you count Matt,* she added silently. "Matt wanted to have a nanny on staff, too, but I said I wanted to be the one to take care of Cody." She'd had to fight him tooth and nail on that, but that one time he'd backed down, throwing up his hands and muttering that she was crazy but so be it. "It would have been different if I'd worked," she explained, not wanting to make Matt out to be an ogre. He had been, after all, Cody's father. "But he really didn't want me to do that."

Her voice was mild, but Trent caught the tense undercurrent. He wondered when her marriage had begun to disintegrate. Keeping an even, friendly tone, he asked, "What did he want you to do?"

Again she shrugged, as if what she said made no difference to her. But he heard the hurt. "Be there when he wanted me," she said quietly.

Trent read between the lines. "And that wasn't very often?"

Ever private, a protest rose to her lips. She began to say no, then raised her eyes to his. He'd know if she was lying. He had that knack. But she didn't want him there, didn't want him seeing her regrets. It was too late to act on them and having him see only compounded the matter.

"You're Cody's therapist, Trent, not mine," she reminded him tersely.

"I'm not being a therapist right now," he assured her.

"Then what?"

"A friend," he told her gently. "I'm being a friend. I thought you might be able to use one."

She had no idea how the distance between them had dissolved, no idea how she'd wound up in his arms, her face pressed against his chest as she struggled to hold back the tears. She only knew she was here, and that Trent held her. And that somehow, just for the moment, her demons were at bay.

"You're right," she whispered. "I can."

Chapter Nine

Laurel lengthened her stride to keep from falling behind. Because it was spring break, Knott's Berry Farm's hours began earlier than usual and they had been here since the gates had opened.

Throughout the first few hours, she kept glancing at Cody's face, hoping for some indication that this "field trip" would be the key that would finally open the glass prison that surrounded her son. That magically he would turn into the little boy she'd brought here about fourteen months ago.

A lifetime ago.

Back then Cody's bright blue eyes had been as big as saucers as he had tried to take in everything at once. Eighty percent of the park looked like weathered scenes from the

Wild West and Cody had just discovered cowboys, thanks to an old John Wayne movie on the classic movie channel. His usual gusto for life had all but doubled and he'd been completely enthralled.

But when they'd arrived here this morning, that enthusiasm had been conspicuously absent. His face expressionless, it was as if Cody were sleepwalking through the experience.

The stagecoach ride they took, with Cody seated on top, next to the driver, did nothing to change his demeanor.

Neither did the old-fashioned train ride, a rickety fifteen-minute trip, complete with a set of train robbers who bantered with the passengers they were pretending to rob. When one of the robbers attempted to draw Cody into the scenario, the boy merely stared at him. The "robber," sensing something was wrong, quickly moved on to another boy.

Laurel sighed as they got off the train. It was a noble plan, but it wasn't working.

She watched Trent swing the little boy off the metal step between the coupled cars and place him down onto the ground.

The magic she'd once felt here was gone. "Maybe we should go home," she suggested.

Trent looked at her, mild surprise in his eyes. "Why?"

She leaned in closer, lowering her voice. "It's not working and there's no reason for you to waste the rest of your day."

"I've got no place else to be," he told Laurel. "Do you?"

Two children holding half-eaten cones of cotton candy raced by her, ahead of their parents. She stepped aside to avoid a collision. "No."

"Then, since we're here, we might as well stay," Trent said philosophically. He thought a moment. "Did Cody have a favorite ride here?"

Laurel laughed softly. "The log ride," she told him.

Damp from the spray that had hit them as the "log" they were riding in had splashed into the water, she and Cody would get off and run to the end of the line, ready for another ride. He couldn't seem to get his fill of it. And each and every time, Cody had clutched her hand excitedly, squeezing it and shrieking with joy as they had ridden the log down a thirty-foot plunge.

What she wouldn't give to have that back.

"All right, then we'll hit the log ride," Trent declared. "And after that, the petting zoo." He turned to look at the boy. "Does that sound good to you, Cody? The log ride and then the petting zoo?" As he asked, he watched Cody's face closely for any sign of a connection.

Cody raised his eyes from the ground and looked at him. And then there was just the smallest, almost imperceptible inclination of his head.

"That's a yes," Trent announced, slanting a look in Laurel's direction.

Taking Cody's hand as if it were the most natural thing in the world, Trent placed his other hand against Laurel's back to guide her. With both in tow, he hurried them along through the park, crossing the tracks before the train that was just moments from another run through "the badlands."

Quickening her pace, Laurel felt a lump in her throat. God help her, but she felt as if they were a unit. A family. If only life had "do overs," she knew which moment she would choose.

But despite Trent's patience and kindness, in her heart she felt that he would never forgive her for hurting him. Not just because she'd turned him down and disappeared, but because she'd then married someone else. The very act had been like a slap in the face for him, especially in light of the circumstances. Her reason for not saying yes to him was because, ultimately, she was haunted by what had happened to her as a child.

A little girl was supposed to trust her father, be protected by her father. If she couldn't rely on him, if he turned out to be the very one who physically and emotionally hurt her instead of being there for her, how could she trust any other man? Trent had accepted this on some level.

But how could he accept the fact that after everything, she had turned around and married Matt less than six months later? She wasn't about to tell Trent why she had done it because that would be making excuses for herself. Moreover, she saw it as begging him to understand, and she couldn't beg, not for herself.

For Cody was another matter.

And despite the shadow in their past, Trent was coming through for Cody, wasn't he?

I wish I'd had a little more faith in you—and my heart,

back then, Trent. Things would have turned out very differently.

The line for the log ride was long, snaking around the perimeter of the so-called "lake" where the logs came down from the flume. But for the moment, the line moved rather quickly. They made their way up along the outside of the "mountainside" until they finally came to stand before the hollowed-out mock logs.

"Keep moving, keep moving," an attendant in the red flannel shirt, jeans, woolen cap and high-laced leather boots urged, waving the three of them into a vacant log. "One in back, two in front." He guided Trent to take a seat in the rear and thus balance out their weight.

Trent got in, then extended his hand to Laurel to help her into the log. Once inside, Laurel helped her son in, as they all took their seats almost simultaneously.

Sitting inside the rectangular, narrow space was far from comfortable. Trent's long legs formed a parenthesis around hers, and her legs in turn stretched on either side of Cody to buffer the jolting ride.

Trent's legs being around hers, however, didn't serve as a buffer as much as an igniter. Having Trent so close to her, his legs pressed against hers, his torso right up against her back, brought every single nerve ending in her body to rapt attention. Feelings were going on inside of her that had absolutely no safe outlet.

Laurel took in a deep breath, bracing herself. She did what she could to focus on the ride, desperately trying not to think about the man behind her.

She would have been more successful if she'd just decided to stop breathing.

As the log inched its way through the inside of a cave, highlighting what the life of a miner must have been like a hundred and fifty years ago, Laurel closed her arms around Cody's waist.

For once, she didn't feel her son stiffening when she touched him.

Thank you, Trent!

The log sped up, going faster and faster as it dipped and rose, traveling down the engineered rapids. And then suddenly they were back to inching along. But this time the log was going up and up, all within an expanse of semidarkness.

The creak of the mechanism's chains only made the prospect of what was to come more nerve-racking. All around them, children squealed in anticipation. All but her child.

Their log arrived at the apex, its progress halted for a long split second. Laurel, in the middle, could feel the log teetering on the brink.

And then, without warning, they were plunging down a steep decline, racing toward a man-made body of water below.

Laurel felt her stomach rise up in her throat, felt Trent's arms closing around her waist more tightly even as she tightened her own hold on Cody. All three of them were buckled down in their seats, but the feeling that any moment they could go flying out of the ride seemed like a very real possibility.

She screamed to release her built-up tension. Her voice

mingled with those of all the other riders. In front of her as well as directly behind her, they were doing the same thing. Screaming at the top of their lungs.

It took her less than an agitated heartbeat to realize that Cody was screaming, too.

She had to restrain herself from tightening her hold around his waist. If she squeezed him any harder, she would have cut off his air supply. Joy bounced erratically through her.

All right, Cody wasn't talking—yet. But this was at least another, louder sound than he had been making. That was progress, right?

It was to her.

Laurel didn't even realize they'd gotten wet until the log had slowed down considerably and the mechanisms beneath it had pulled it up to the unloading zone.

Trent hopped out first, then held out one hand to her and the other to Cody. There was no hesitation on Cody's part. He took Trent's hand and quickly clambered out of the log.

"Well, that was a lot more exciting than I remember it," Trent commented, brushing the water droplets out of his hair. When he and Laurel had frequented this park, there had been fewer logs, but he hadn't minded waiting. Hadn't minded being anywhere as long as he was with her. Grinning, he turned his attention to Cody. "I feel like doing this a second time. How about it, Cody? Are you game? Do you want to do it again?"

Instead of answering, Cody was already hurrying to find the end of the line.

Trent gave Laurel an encouraging smile and winked. "Looks like we're getting on that ride again."

In total, they went on the ride another five times before, soaked, they decided it was time to test out another, drier ride.

But not before Laurel stopped at the photography booth where she could purchase a print of the picture the camera perched overlooking the top of the flume had taken of them. The selection ranged from several different sizes of prints to a key chain. She bought a key chain and a five-by-seven print, wanting to press this moment between the pages of time.

"We're both screaming," Laurel said, studying the photograph as she walked away from the booth. She referred to Cody and her. "But you look as if you're laughing." She looked at Trent. Most of the people in the other photos projected on a screen next to the booth were screaming, too. Which made him a loner. "Why?"

"Because I was having a good time," he said simply. There'd been no bubble of tension within his chest. The only thing humming within was a sense of happiness. And that he didn't want to release. He wanted to hang on to that feeling as long as possible.

"Okay, everyone set to hit the petting zoo?" he asked, once Laurel had tucked away the photo and her key chain. He thought he heard one of their stomachs rumble in protest. "Or would you guys like to stop to get something to eat first?"

"I could eat," Laurel told him. Until he'd made the suggestion, she hadn't realized just how hungry she'd become. She'd been too focused on Cody, too happy about his progress.

"And you?" Trent asked Cody.

Cody looked undecided whether to acknowledge the question. And then, just as Trent was about to turn away, the boy nodded his head.

"Lunch it is," Trent declared in triumph. "Let's go." Again, taking the boy's hand, he began to weave his way through the colorful, crowded streets.

Bringing up the rear, Laurel noted with no small pleasure that Cody didn't seem as if he wanted to pull his hand away from Trent's.

The man was a miracle worker, she thought. There was no other way to describe it. She would have never thought of coming here if Trent hadn't suggested it. And now look, Cody had made another stride.

She hadn't been wrong in seeking out Trent to ask for help. She just hoped that having him back in her life temporarily wouldn't leave any permanent repercussions.

Who was she kidding? It already had. But it was too late for regrets. What was done was done. She had to move forward. She had to think about Cody.

The moment they reached the restaurant in the middle of the park, she recognized it. They had always come here during their past trips to the park. With effort, she shut away the memories. There was no point in reliving them. She knew how the story ended.

The restaurant, whose open kitchen looked like a chuck

wagon with its cover pulled back and its wooden ribs exposed, was filling up quickly. They secured the last available table. Behind them, a line of waiting patrons started to form.

The waitress came by with three glasses of water and an order pad. Laurel had taken a quick glance at the menu. It hadn't changed in eight years, although the prices had gone up accordingly. She placed her order. Trent was next, ordering a duplicate of hers.

Then he looked at Cody. "Your turn, champ." Cody sat there, looking back at him.

"I can come back," the waitress offered.

"No, this'll just take another minute," Trent assured her. Patiently, Trent held up a menu before the boy, flipping to the children's page. "C'mon, Cody, I need a hint," he urged softly.

Pressing his small lips together, Cody scanned the menu before him, then pointed to an item.

Turning it so that he could see what had captured the boy's attention, Trent read, "Giant ribs." The serving, he knew, was going to be half as big as Cody was tall. He did his best to keep his lips from twitching into a smile. Instead, he solemnly nodded his approval.

"Good choice," he proclaimed. Closing the menu, he handed it to the waitress. "Cody would like a serving of giant ribs."

The young woman eyed the boy dubiously. "You sure?"

Trent made eye contact with Cody, then told the waitress, "He's sure."

She shook her head, but wrote down the order. "Okay." And then she looked up, her pen still poised. "What kind of veggies?"

"French fries?" Trent asked Cody. Cody nodded.

He was good with the boy, Laurel thought, another pang squeezing her heart. Not for the first time she thought that if she had jumped over the hurdle that her fear had constructed and married Trent when he'd asked, Cody would have been their son. And he wouldn't have been trapped in a car with his dead father. Everything would have turned out differently.

Noting the solemn, faraway look in Laurel's eyes, after the waitress had departed, Trent leaned in and asked, "Something wrong?"

"No," she answered, her eyes shifting from him to Cody. She forced a smile to her lips. "Something's right. Very right."

Trent knew better than to press.

"Are you really planning on carrying that doggie bag around for the duration of the day?" Laurel asked nearly an hour later, as they walked out of the restaurant.

Both she and Trent had done justice to their meals and easily finished them. Cody's lunch, however, was a different story. He'd consumed all his French fries, which, given the fact that he wasn't a big eater, had taken up a lot of space inside his stomach. He had hardly eaten a quarter of his main course. Trent had asked the waitress to pack up the rest.

Trent looked down at the brown bag he held. One side had developed a greasy oval spot the size of a baseball.

"Hey, good ribs are good ribs," he told her. Catching Cody's eye, he winked, as if they shared a secret. "And you never know. We might get stranded on our way back home. These ribs could easily make the difference between life and death."

She laughed, shaking her head. "If you say so, Trent."

Their next stop was the petting zoo. The fenced-off enclosure was stocked with baby animals that ranged from rabbits, piglets and goats to a miniature Shetland pony. Children who met the age and height requirement were accompanied by their parents, who provided protection—whether for the children or the animals was a little unclear. They also purchased the pellets that the animals were allowed to eat.

Wanting Cody to be more than a passive observer, Laurel dug through her purse for the proper change. After locating coins, she inserted them into the dispenser, turned the metal knob and then cupped Cody's hand beneath the mouth of the machine. Lifting the cover, tiny, unappetizing-looking beige pellets belched out of the dispenser's mouth. Cody raised a quizzical eyebrow as he regarded the pellets.

He didn't remember, she thought. "You feed those to the animals. That way, they're easier to pet," she encouraged.

A goat wandered up, momentarily drawn to Cody's bounty—but then another, far more tempting aroma caught his attention. In the blink of an eye, the baby goat, as well as several of his brethren and friends, closed in around Trent, surrounding him.

"I think you've got competition for those ribs," she told Trent with a laugh.

Holding the bag aloft over his head, Trent began to inch his way over to the gate. The goats followed. He glanced back at Laurel.

"I think you might have something there," Trent agreed.

Not about to be denied, and most likely sick of pellets, the goats became more aggressive. The ones closest to Trent gave chase.

Speeding up, Trent made it to the gate and managed to close it behind him just in time. But not before the goat that had led the others in the pursuit of ribs managed to butt him.

Some of the other children watched and began to laugh.

As did Cody.

Laurel's eyes met Trent's. Hers were wide with excitement. Cody was laughing. She'd given up hope that she would hear that wonderful, infectious sound ever again.

Trent placed a finger to his lips, indicating that she wasn't to call attention to the change in Cody's usual solemn demeanor. Laurel pressed her lips together. It wasn't easy containing her excitement, or her delight, but she managed.

The only giveaway was the huge, wide smile that curved her lips.

Chapter Ten

Enveloped in night, the car's smooth ride had all but rocked her to sleep. Laurel struggled to rouse herself. Taking a deep breath, she sat up straighter, adjusting her seat belt's shoulder strap to move it away from the side of her neck where it had slipped.

They were almost home.

Twisting around, she looked into the backseat. Cody was sound asleep. Peace descended over her. When she saw him like that, she could almost pretend that everything was all right, that this was still the little boy who loved to run and play.

"That was wonderful," she said to Trent in a soft voice. "When you first suggested it, I didn't think it was a very good idea." Lord, but she was glad Trent hadn't listened to her protest. “But he really started coming around today, didn’t he?”

Trent pulled up in her driveway and switched off the ignition. “We’re still pretty far from the goalpost, but getting there.” It was obvious that he was pleased with how the outing had turned out.

Getting out of his car, Trent rounded the hood and paused to open her door, then Cody’s. He leaned in and released the belts holding Cody in place. Very gently, he picked the boy up in his arms.

“I can do that,” Laurel told him, moving so that she was beside him.

But rather than transfer the boy into her arms, Trent continued to hold him. “No problem. Cody’s not exactly a big, husky kid,” he noted, his mouth curving. And then he raised his eyes to her face. “Takes after his mom that way.”

Both she and Cody were small-boned. She laughed softly as she fell into step beside Trent. “It frustrated him, being the smallest in his kindergarten class. He wanted to be like his father. Tall and athletic. I told him he’d grow into it.”

Her smile turned sad as she stopped by the front door. Trent thought it was because she missed her late husband. But her next words told him her mind was elsewhere.

“It all sounds so normal, doesn’t it?”

There was longing in her voice. He knew what she was thinking. She didn’t miss Matt. She missed the way Cody had been before the accident.

“It will be again,” Trent told her. Unconsciously, he

drew the sleeping boy closer to him, as if he could somehow transfer his own tranquility to Cody. "I promise."

Laurel pressed the keypad next to the door, disarming the security system before she inserted her key into the lock and opened the door. She entered first.

"You can't promise that," she told him. Laurel shut the door behind Trent. "You don't know that he'll ever come around." She'd been trying to educate herself about Cody's condition ever since Trent had begun working with him. "I read a case study the other day online that said—"

He turned toward her with Cody still nestled in his arms. About half of the information online was actually accurate. He didn't want her to be misled.

"Stop reading," Trent advised her. "Every case is different. Cody will come around. I'm not going to give up on him." It was a solemn, unshakable promise.

She believed him. Not just because she wanted to, but because Trent was as good as his word. He always had been. "I don't know how to thank you." How do you begin to thank the person who saves your child?

"You don't have to," he told her simply. "It's my job. It's what I do. What I am."

Her mouth curved. "A patron saint to lost children and their parents?"

His eyes took on a twinkle as humor filled them. "I wouldn't exactly go that far—but you can if you want to." And then he looked at her more closely. Shadows began to form beneath her eyes. "You look tired, Laurel."

"It *was* a long day," she reminded him and, except for

the rides and the trip home, the entire time had been spent on her feet. It was taxing, keeping up not with Cody but with Trent.

"Why don't you stay down here?" he suggested. Trent nodded at the child in his arms. "I'll go put him to bed."

Laurel opened her mouth to protest. After all, Cody was her son, her responsibility. But Trent was already heading toward the spiral staircase. For a moment, she just stood and watched him, holding back a flood of emotions that threatened to undo her.

A bittersweet feeling pervaded Trent as he carried Laurel's son up the stairs. He truly liked children, liked helping them, but the idea of having his own had never crossed his mind. Not since Laurel had vanished from his life. Because before children, there had to be a woman he loved, a woman he wanted to spend the rest of his life with, have children with and share both laughter and tears.

There was no such woman in his life. Not anymore.

For the most part, when it came to matchmaking, Kate and his father had pretty much left him alone. But both Mike and Trevor had better halves now. While he was very fond of both his sisters-in-law, Miranda and Venus thought it was part of their responsibility to find a suitable match for him.

Miranda would invite him over for dinner and, likely as not, a fourth place at the table would be occupied by some woman from the science community, where most of her friends were. Venus did the same, except that her friends were women whose faces on occasion graced the society pages of the L.A. *Times*.

All in all, there'd been a bevy of interesting women, even beautiful women, but not once had he felt the slightest spark of electricity.

There never had been that chemistry between him and a woman. Except for once.

"And that was your mother," he murmured out loud, addressing his words to the sleeping boy as he placed him on top of the comforter.

Very carefully, he removed the boy's sneakers and socks, putting them side by side on the floor next to the bed. He thought of getting the boy into pajamas, but he had a feeling that might wake up Cody. It was more important to let him continue sleeping. So instead of undressing him further, Trent took the end of the comforter and lightly covered the boy.

For a moment, he just stood there, looking at Cody. Sleeping, the boy looked a great deal like his mother, Trent thought, an ache slipping into his chest. When he finally turned away, he found himself all but walking into Laurel, who stood in the doorway, apparently watching both of them.

She nodded toward the sleeping boy, amusement curving the corners of her mouth. "You sleep in your clothes, too?"

"Only when I'm too exhausted to change." That had happened on a couple of occasions, back in his college days when he'd been cramming for a major exam on the next day. "I was afraid putting him into his pajamas might wake him up."

"He is a light sleeper," she confirmed, and then she

smiled. Trent just always inherently seemed to do the right thing. "Good instincts."

"Sometimes," he allowed.

Instantly, she knew he was talking about her. Or maybe that was just her paranoia spiking. Laurel quietly eased the bedroom door shut, then followed Trent downstairs.

It seemed that lately she was always trying to keep down feelings that threatened to erupt. Seeing Trent again had stirred up so many emotions, causing her to revisit memories better left in the shadows.

He was getting ready to leave. She could tell by his body language. It was late and he'd done more than enough for her, but she didn't want to see him go. Not just yet. She didn't want to let this feeling of hope, of well-being, evaporate, at least not for a few more minutes, and it would once Trent went out that door.

She cast about for something to postpone the inevitable.

"Would you like something to drink?" she offered. "Coffee, tea, something with alcohol?"

What he wanted wasn't anything that could be contained in a glass or a cup. The velvet darkness had ushered in some of the old feelings, making him want her. Which was why he knew he had to leave.

"No, thanks. It's late and I'd better get going so that you can get to bed, too."

Lately her nights had been long and drawn out, marked by bouts of sleeplessness. "Don't leave because of that reason," she urged. "I probably won't get much sleep anyway."

She'd piqued his interest. "You have trouble sleeping?"

She shrugged, realizing she shouldn't have said anything. She didn't want Trent thinking she'd become some high-strung, neurotic woman.

"Can't seem to shut down my mind at night." It was at least partially true. "Too much to think about."

He wondered what kept Laurel up at night. Was it just her concern for Cody, or did she regret what might have been between them?

"You could have your doctor prescribe a mild sleeping pill," he suggested. "A lot of new things on the market might help you."

She shook her head. "That's okay. I'd rather not start pumping things into my system like—" Realizing her mistake, Laurel abruptly stopped talking.

She didn't have to finish. He knew what she was about to say.

"Like your mother?" he asked gently.

He didn't know all the details of the story, but in a particularly stressful moment, she had told him that after her mother had thrown her father out and they'd divorced, her mother had started taking pills to get to sleep. Moreover, she had begun to drink to get through the days. Grace Valentine had remained a prisoner of both for more than ten years until she'd finally managed to triumph over her addictions.

Laurel raised her chin. She and her mother had gone through some rough patches, especially after she'd married Matt, but she was devoted to the woman and very protective of her.

"She's still on the wagon," she said defensively.

He smiled, nodding. He knew how much that meant to Laurel. "Good for her."

Nerves began to surface. Maybe it was better that he left now. These feelings she was having would only further complicate things. She could handle one problem at a time, she told herself.

"Thank you again," she said.

His eyes crinkled. "The pleasure was entirely mine, Laurel."

This was where he was supposed to turn on his heel and head out the door. Why he didn't was a testimony to the fact that he was only human. Maybe a little too human.

He caught himself missing Laurel. Missing the feelings that only she was capable of generating within him, even now. Only she had made him willing to risk the heartache and disappointment that lurked within the shadows of a relationship.

Of a marriage.

And how's that working for you? Trent mocked himself.

But common sense proved no deterrent. Trent knew what he was going to do the second he looked into her eyes. It was a foregone conclusion. It was his destiny, karma or whatever the proper term was for the madness that assaulted him.

He had no choice. He *had* to kiss her. *Had* to take hold of her shoulders and bring his mouth down to hers. The moment his lips touched hers, he felt the explosion, felt the rush.

He wanted her—wanted her so badly that he felt if he didn't have her he would self-destruct right here in her grand foyer with its marble floors and seven-tiered crystal chandelier.

Trent deepened the kiss, hardly aware that he was even doing it. Deepened it as his hands slipped from her shoulders and moved up along the sides of her neck to frame her face, touching her as if she were fragile and precious. As if a single wrong move would make her break into a thousand little pieces.

Her head spun. Only Trent could do that to her. Only he could make her blood rush and her pulse race. Only he could make her knees turn to mush. A soft moan escaped her lips as Laurel bent into him. She could feel her body heating.

And then the old demons came back, the ones that had been forged the night her father had come into her room and with one thoughtless, self-centered and cruel act, had ripped her away from her childhood.

No, you can't do this.

Shaking, Laurel pulled back her head. There were tears in her eyes as she looked at him. How could she be afraid of the very thing she yearned for?

"Trent—"

Her tone stopped him far more effectively than any words could. Memories of squelched frustration assaulted him. Nothing had changed. She was still withdrawing from him. Withdrawing from him while she'd given herself to the man she'd married.

Trent took a step back, struggling for composure. “Sorry,” he apologized stiffly. “Told you I should be going.” With that, he walked out.

He’d almost reached his car when he thought he heard her. Turning, he asked, “What did you say?”

Laurel leaned against the doorjamb. The word *nothing* hovered on her lips. But that would have been a lie. He didn’t deserve a lie just because she’d lost her nerve.

Taking a breath, she repeated her words. “It wasn’t that I didn’t love you, you know.”

Out of the many meanings Laurel could have intended, he instinctively knew a lack of love hadn’t been the reason she’d turned down his proposal.

His lips twisted in a bitter smile. “It’s just that you didn’t love me enough.”

She shook her head, struggling to keep tears at bay. She couldn’t feel sorry for herself. Her life had played out a certain way and she had to accept that.

“No, that wasn’t it.” She spoke so softly, she forced him to double back in order to hear her. “I loved you more than I thought I could.” She ran the tip of her tongue over her lips, to moisten them. “I was just afraid.” Laurel raised her eyes to his face. “Afraid to say yes and then disappoint you.” Distress filled her voice. “Afraid that I couldn’t be what you wanted me to be.”

He wouldn’t have put demands on her. Didn’t she know that? He’d loved her too much to bring her pain. “And what is it that you thought I wanted you to be?”

“A wife,” she whispered. A wife and all that entailed.

Because she was frozen inside. So frozen. The little girl whose virginity had been stolen from her had shut down the woman who came to be in her place.

He would have believed her—if it weren't for the fact that she had gotten married so shortly afterward. "And you could for Matt?"

That, too, was something she would always pay for. But there, at least, she had done some good. "That was different."

"How?" Trent asked, his emotions getting the better of him. He raised his voice without realizing it. "How was that different?"

She turned away from him, knotting her fingers together helplessly. She just should have let him leave.

"It just was," she finally said to him, her eyes pleading for understanding if not forgiveness. "It had nothing to do with how I felt about you, I swear it." She pressed her lips together, thinking of how she'd sold herself for a price. "I *had* to marry Matt."

Trent stared at her, not quite processing what she was telling him. Was she telling him— "You were pregnant?" he asked incredulously.

"No." And then she laughed shortly, although there was no humor in the sound. "That was one of the reasons he married me, I think. Because I was such a challenge for him. Because I was a virgin and his ego liked the idea of being first. No one had ever said no to him before." Matt had been so certain that he could make fireworks go off for her. And he had become angry when he saw that he couldn't. To avoid blaming himself, he blamed her.

She closed her eyes, doing her best not to relive the memory.

"But it bothered him that I couldn't respond to him. I tried." Opening her eyes again, she looked at Trent, afraid of seeing pity in his eyes. "I really tried but every time he touched me, I just froze." As she spoke, her breathing grew shallow. "Especially when he became angry and demanding."

But that, she thought, was the nature of the beast. She just hadn't realized it until it was too late.

"Matt was accustomed to getting—or buying—everything he wanted without any opposition, so he wasn't a very patient man. But it got harder instead of easier." A shiver slid up and down her spine. "I cringed inside every time he came to bed. So he stopped coming."

Trent heard what she wasn't saying. "And started spending time with other women?"

She nodded. "Not that Matt needed much of an excuse. I think the women would have come even if I had satisfied him." She tried to shrug off the matter, but he could see that it had hurt her. "He was just that kind of a person. Matt needed to be revered, needed to bask in the light of adoring eyes."

Moved, wishing he could make the pain in her eyes disappear, Trent touched her face ever so lightly. "There is a very hypnotic glow in your eyes right now," he told her, his voice low, seductive. "I could see how a man could get trapped there."

To his surprise, rather than saying something self-deprecating, Laurel threaded her arms around his neck. And then she kissed him.

Kissed him hard.

With feeling.

As if she were desperately trying to outdistance her demons. The ones that so often commandeered her, mind and body, so that she couldn't let herself go. Couldn't allow herself to be his.

Stunned, Trent drew back. Either he was dreaming or had somehow slipped into a parallel universe.

"You might not realize it, but this isn't exactly the right way to say no," he pointed out. A man could only be so strong before all control was torn out of his hands and he became a pawn of his own desires.

"That's because I'm not saying no," she told him breathlessly, a heartbeat before she sealed her lips back to his.

Chapter Eleven

Trent knew he had no option.

He had to save Laurel from herself—even if he was going to hate himself for this in the morning.

Hell, what morning? He wasn't all that delighted with himself right now. But he knew that Laurel was exceptionally vulnerable and he couldn't take advantage of that, couldn't, only because of a weak moment. It just wouldn't be right.

So, hard as it was, he gently removed her arms from around his neck and drew his mouth away from hers. He could feel everything inside of him shouting in protest. He continued to hold her hands in his as he searched her face for his own answers.

"Laurel, are you sure?"

"I can sign a waiver if you want," she told him flippantly. And then she stopped as a thought came rushing at her. "Unless you don't want me—"

How could she have been so stupid as to think he'd still want her after all this time? He'd moved on. Any normal person would have. Life didn't freeze-frame just because she wanted it to.

She wasn't prepared to hear him laugh in response. "Now, that's funny."

"Funny?" she repeated stiffly, shriveling up inside.

"Yes, funny." How could she even remotely think that he didn't want her? Hadn't she felt anything when they'd kissed? Hadn't she felt his longing? It wasn't for his sake he was pushing her away, it was for hers. "Because I have wanted you for a very long time," he admitted quietly. And then, because this was Laurel, he bared his soul to her. "I actually thought I was over you. Until I saw you again. And then I realized that all I had managed to do was bury my feelings." And they had come back—in spades. He sighed, resigned to his fate. "But they're not gone and they're not dead. They're still there, waiting for one of us to come to our senses."

One of us? She shook her head, confused. "I don't understand."

"My coming to my senses would be finally accepting that it's never going to happen between us." And then he smiled again. "You coming to your senses would mean that you realized that you wanted to be with me all along and that you'd made a mistake turning me down when I proposed."

She didn't want to stand there, philosophizing or trying to solve some theoretical puzzle. She wanted Trent to break down her barriers, wanted him to make her feel whole for the first time in her life. Because if anyone could do it, it was Trent.

More than anything else in the world, she wanted desperately to feel like a real woman instead of just a two-dimensional paper cutout. Without fear, without demons.

Taking a breath, Laurel wrapped her arms around his neck again, bringing her body tantalizingly close to his, the heat all but sealing them together. Her eyes pleaded her case before she said anything.

"Make love to me, Trent."

His mouth curved as he slowly shook his head. "Now, right there," he told her gently, "you've got it all wrong."

"Wrong?" What was she getting wrong? Was he going to make her beg? Because she would if she had to. Just this once, she would.

He nodded in response to the single word she echoed. "I'm not going to make love to you, Laurel."

Her heart stood still, and then began to slowly splinter. "You're not?" she heard herself ask, her voice echoing in her head.

"No, I'm not," he told her. Releasing her hands, he slipped his around her waist. "I'm going to make love *with* you."

She felt like a ball in play at a tennis match. "You're confusing me."

The key word here was *with* and he could see that she'd missed its importance. "We're partners here, Laurel. You're not some vessel meant to satisfy me, not some life-size, plastic blow-up doll for me to do things to."

Trent was trying to keep his adrenaline in check, but it was far from easy. This was something that he'd wanted, dreamed of, for a very long time. But just as he hadn't pushed his advantage years ago, he wasn't about to do it now. Her emotional well-being was at stake and he cared too much about her to sacrifice it.

"Lovemaking," he told Laurel, "is a mutual experience."

As he spoke, Trent began to kiss the side of her neck ever so lightly, first one side, then the other. The sound of her sharply drawing in her breath only served to excite him. He had to restrain himself to keep from upping the tempo. Timing, he knew, was everything, and anything worth having was worth waiting for.

And he had waited for this for a very, very long time.

Laurel felt as if she were on fire.

Sheets of warmth rose up within her, beginning at her knees and traveling upward until she was almost certain she was shooting flames from the tips of her hair.

She twisted against Trent, leaning into him, into the wild, exhilarating magic that his mouth created for her. Desire took root within her, making her want more.

She felt his hands on her, not roughly, or possessively, like Matt before he'd stopped coming to her, but ever so gently. His fingers and palms just barely touched her at first, moving along the length of her as if to memorize every inch.

Laurel felt herself heating, responding.

She'd never experienced this before. A dampness in her inner core, a desire that broke out of its bonds. There was a rushing sound in her ears, as if she were going down for the third time, being towed under by a giant, overpowering wave.

And then his mouth was on hers, kissing her so that he drew the very essence from her, melting her into a formless being.

Laurel literally clung to him to keep from slipping to the floor.

She felt Trent smiling against her lips.

Did she amuse him? Despite the fact that she was no longer a virgin, did her lack of sophistication entertain Trent?

Laurel broke contact, although even with the negative thoughts erupting in her head, it wasn't easy. "You're laughing at me," she said hoarsely.

"I'm enjoying you," he contradicted. There was a very good reason for him to be smiling, even as his lips were otherwise occupied. "I never thought this day would come."

Struggling to collect himself, to think logically in the midst of this delicious tempest, he looked toward the staircase. They were out in the open here—where Cody could see them if he woke up. Trent couldn't predict how the boy would react to seeing his mother kissing someone else and he certainly didn't want the boy to see anything more.

He gave her a way out—one last time. And fervently prayed she wouldn't take it. "If you want this to continue, we need to go to your room."

"If I want this to continue," she echoed. He made it sound as if she were the only one who was feeling something. She put the question to him. "If I said no, you'd just walk away?"

How could he make her understand? "There's no 'just' to it, but I'd walk away, yes."

Her heart sank. "Then you don't feel anything?"

He searched her face. "Is that what you think?"

She fought back tears. "What else am I supposed to think?"

"That I'm not a rutting pig, that I don't see you as having been put on this earth just to satisfy my basic needs." A surge of anger spiked through him because she put him in the same category as the men who had failed her. Didn't she know he was different? "That I respect you enough to withdraw and be miserably frustrated if you don't want me to go on."

He was saying all the right things. Now she struggled not to cry for a different reason.

"I want you to go on," she told him, her voice so soft he had to lean in to hear her.

Then, so that there was no doubt in his mind, Laurel took his hand and led the way up the stairs. She congratulated herself on making it to the landing without her knees buckling. This was a huge step for her and she couldn't pretend that she wasn't afraid.

But she was even more afraid of not doing it.

Still holding him by the hand, she led Trent into the master bedroom. The bedroom she had briefly shared with Matt until, disgusted, he had opted for separate sleeping arrangements.

Her eyes on his, Laurel held her breath as she slowly pushed the door closed.

The sound of the lock clicking into place echoed in her head.

They were alone.

Together.

This was really going to happen.

Her hands turned icy. She could feel her heart hammering, its tempo increasing.

"I have to tell you something," Laurel began, just as he started to take her into his arms.

Braced for anything, he had no idea what to expect. "Go ahead."

Summoning her courage, she blurted the words out. "I haven't done…this…very much since Cody was born." Pausing, she pressed her lips together before continuing. He needed to know this so that he wouldn't expect too much from her. "Matt said I was frigid and not worth the trouble."

Matt grew steadily more despicable in his eyes. Trent couldn't help commenting, "Sounds like Matt was one hell of a winner." It was difficult to refrain from asking why she'd married the man to begin with.

She shrugged in response, not knowing what to say. Matt had been right in his assessment. She *was* frigid. The moment he put his hands on her, the second he dragged her over to him, something inside of her wanted to retreat. To run. And it annoyed the hell out of him.

Very slowly, slipping his hands along her face, Trent began kissing her again. Starting not where he had left off downstairs, but from scratch, as if she had to be won all over again.

As if he were taking nothing for granted just because she'd brought him up here.

He wasn't kissing her as if he knew they were destined to make love, she realized. He kissed her as if he had no idea where this would lead, only knowing that he enjoyed the moment. Immensely.

As did she, Laurel realized with joy, her pulse racing wildly.

Fear, ever her companion, pricked at the edges of her consciousness. But for once it was being blocked. Blocked by a wall of flame as Trent's strong hands languidly roamed over her body. Her temperature rose steadily.

She burned for him.

That first night, after the wedding, Matt had all but ripped off her clothes, saying something about wanting to finally see what he had paid for. It was a crude reference to the fact that he'd paid for her mother's surgery, as she'd asked. It had made her feel dirty, cheap. As if she'd sold herself. Because, in effect, she had.

Despite her feelings, she'd done her best to keep her end of the bargain. But she had no experience when it came to this frontier. Because of her past, her only framework was pain—and fear.

Matt pleasured himself with her that first night without a single word of endearment. She might as well have not been there, at least not in spirit. Without anything else to go on, Laurel half expected the same from Trent, and that did scare her. But she had no other way to express her thanks for everything he'd done for her son, and she'd sensed that this was what he wanted. And she wanted to please him.

She hadn't expected to be blown away.

Hadn't expected to feel anything but the desire for this to be over.

The wild, erratic sensations just kept coming in overpowering waves, completely disorienting her. Trent's open-mouth kisses along her skin wreaked havoc on her resistance. Making it a thing of the past.

Completely stunned, Laurel felt her body yearning for him. But as he slowly drew her clothes away from her skin, exposing more and more of her to his touch, she felt warmer, not colder. Felt a strange, exciting urgency grip her, demanding release.

She'd never experienced this before. She could almost feel her blood surging through her veins, rushing throughout her body. And yet, it all seemed to center in her very core.

Her eyes flew open as she felt the onslaught of an exhilarating explosion. Wide-eyed, stunned, she stared at him, speechless.

Whatever this was, it was wonderful!

His smile imprinted itself on her lips as he kissed her mouth. He knew what was happening by the look of wonder in her eyes, by the way her body had arched and bucked against him.

"This is a first, isn't it?" he asked softly.

Laurel had all but scrunched the comforter with grasping hands as she scrambled to catch just a little more of the powerful eruption. She moved her head up and down, her eyes on his.

"Yes," she whispered.

He liked being the first to bring her to this plateau of absolute pleasure. Not because it fed his ego, but because it awarded them a shared intimacy that Laurel had never had with another man.

"We'll see if we can do it again for you," Trent murmured.

He brought his mouth down on hers once more and went on making love with her, his clever hands bringing her ecstasy that went on forever.

Just when she fell back, exhausted, Trent would find a new way to arouse her and the eruptions within her began building all over again. She rode wave after wave, struggling to go on breathing even as joy and triumph ricocheted through her.

She'd never dreamed that these kinds of sensations existed.

And then, finally, when she felt as if the last ounce of strength had been wrenched from her, Trent shifted his position so that his body covered hers.

But unlike when Matt had moved in to claim his final moment, there was no oppressive weight, no struggle for her to catch her breath. Trent pivoted his weight on his elbows so that his body barely touched hers. This teased her almost unmercifully.

Wanting full contact so badly, Laurel arched her torso up to his.

Trent threaded his fingers through hers, bringing their joined hands above her head a beat before he sheathed himself within her.

Kissing her over and over again, he wove his magic as before. And then, sealed together, he moved, at first slowly, gently, taking his time before he increased the tempo.

Had her mouth not been against his, she would have gasped as the sensations mounted. There they were again. She raced to keep up, her hips echoing the movement of his. Sealed together, they sprinted forward to that one beautiful place where euphoria erupted over them in a swift, drenching shower.

Another climax rocked her body, this one so strong, so deep that she bit down on her lower lip to keep from shouting out in elation.

And then, like sunshine ebbing into a receding sunset, the exhilaration faded away, slipped through her fingers and her soul, until it was all but gone, leaving behind only a wonderful memory.

Wow.

The single word echoed over and over again in her brain.

Dazed beyond belief, Laurel took in a deep breath, then let it out slowly, trying to calm her rapid pulse.

She turned her head to look at him, the man who had, at long last, unlocked her prison door. "I didn't realize that it could be like this," she admitted honestly.

"Because no one took the trouble to do it right," he told her simply.

Besides him, Trent thought, she had only had one other partner. Why hadn't her husband taken the time to help her through this and show her what good lovemaking was all about? Caring about your partner, doing what you could to give pleasure was what true lovemaking was about.

He raised himself up on his elbow, looking down at her. "No offense to your late husband, but he sounds like a jerk."

She looked away. "It wasn't his fault."

"Everyone who's a jerk should take responsibility for being one," he pointed out. He had no patience with self-centered people and, from all that he had gleaned, Matt Greer had been the poster boy for narcissism. "He should have been gentle with you."

Matt should have been a lot of things, she couldn't help thinking. But the man was dead and there was no point in speaking ill of him. It didn't change anything. "He didn't know."

Trent's eyebrows drew together in confusion. "About what your father did?"

She continued to look at the far wall. She didn't want to think about her father. All she wanted to do was savor what had just happened a little bit longer. "I never told Matt about my father."

Trent stared at her. How could she have married someone she hadn't trusted enough to share with him the main traumatic event of her childhood? It took everything he had not to ask her why she'd married the man, why, once married, she'd kept her secret to herself.

Instead, Trent merely said, "He still should have gone slowly."

What was done was done. "I don't want to talk about Matt," she told him.

All right, he could understand that. That was then, this was now. Shifting gears, he wound his finger through a strand of her hair that rested against her breast. Ever so lightly, he drew his fingertip along her skin. "So, what do you want to talk about?"

Desire flared in her eyes. "I don't want to talk at all."

Slipping his finger from the curl, he put his hand onto the swell of her hips and gently pulled her to him.

"Your wish is my command," he murmured, just before he kissed her and began the whole wild ride all over again.

Chapter Twelve

The moment she opened the door to admit Trent, Laurel stepped back to get out of the way. With his arms laden with various paraphernalia, Trent's face was hardly visible.

Surprised, she watched as item after item rained down from his arms onto the marble floor. "What *is* all that?" she asked. She looked at the last item he set down. "Is that a tent?"

"That's a tent," he confirmed cheerfully. He knew he should have just carried it all to the back, but he wanted to take a breather. And he couldn't kiss her if she couldn't get close to him. Acting on his thought, he brushed his lips against hers. "And the rest of all this is camping gear."

Besides the tent, there was a lantern, rolled-up sleeping bags, miscellaneous things she didn't even begin to recognize, and on his back a knapsack stuffed to capacity.

She looked at him, puzzled. "Did I miss something? Are we going camping?"

Laurel tried not to frown as she asked the question. If pressed, she'd admit that she really wasn't into roughing it. The idea of sleeping on the hard, insect-infested ground didn't thrill her, although, for Trent, she would be willing to give it a try.

"'We' aren't," he informed her, removing the knapsack from his back and dropping it on the floor beside the rest of the supplies. "Cody and I are."

"You're taking Cody on a camping trip?"

He wondered if she realized just how wide her eyes had opened. For a moment, he thought of stringing her along for a little bit, teasing her, but took pity on her.

"Just to the backyard," he qualified.

She took a deep breath as relief flooded her.

"The backyard?" she asked.

"It might not have occurred to you, but your backyard is the size of a small park." He'd thought of it the other day, remembering that Kate had taken them "camping" in the backyard when he was a kid. He'd had a great time pretending. "I thought this was the best way to break him in for camping. This way, if Cody decides he doesn't like it, we're only several yards away from home."

Drawn by the sound of his voice, Cody had paused his video game and peered out of the family room. Curiosity shone in his eyes when he raised them toward Trent.

Trent saw him immediately. "Cody, just the guy I wanted to see." He beckoned the boy over and Cody crossed to him without hesitation. After two months of interacting with him, Cody no longer hung back. Every tiny step forward was a reason for rejoicing. "What do you say we camp out in your backyard tonight?" Trent asked, draping his arm over the boy's small shoulders. He painted an idyllic picture. "We can roast hot dogs and marshmallows and tell ghost stories." Tilting his head back, Cody looked up at him. Trent could almost read his thoughts. "Right, I'll tell ghost stories, you listen. Sound good?" Cody nodded. "Well, then, let's get started. Grab that knapsack," he instructed, picking up the tent and the poles again.

Overcoming the urge to come to her son's aid, she felt a little useless. "Anything I can do?" Laurel asked Trent.

"Just grab something and fall in," Trent advised, leading the way to the rear of the house.

She picked up the sleeping bags, noting that there were only two, and hurried after Trent and her son.

A little more than an hour later, at dusk, Laurel stood behind the sliding-glass door that led into the backyard. Some distance away, Cody and Trent were sitting on the ground, cross-legged, consuming the "dinner" that Trent had made for them in the barbecue pit.

She felt lonely.

To be fair, Trent had invited her to join them, but she'd demurred, thinking that it might be better if he and Cody had this time together.

Like a father and son.

The words evoked bittersweet feelings. If she'd said yes to Trent all those years ago, then Cody might have been his. And if—

She stopped herself, suppressing a sigh. There was no point in going there. All the *ifs* in the world weren't going to change a thing. The best she could hope for was to learn from her mistakes.

Had she learned anything these last two months?

Other than the fact that her heart rate sped up as she waited for Trent to come up her front walk.

Yes, yes she had, Laurel decided. She'd learned that, under the right circumstances, lovemaking actually could be pleasurable. She hadn't known that before, hadn't believed it possible. She'd learned that she could relax and not be rigid as a stick when a man touched her.

And she'd learned, too, that not all men were created equal. There were differences in the way they behaved in those private, intimate moments.

Up until now, the men in her life had made her believe otherwise.

Her father had been a sick man who by rights should have spent the rest of his days in prison. But he'd managed to escape just before his trial, disappearing into thin air. Because her mother had insisted, Donald Valentine had been tried, convicted and given the maximum sentence for the crime in absentia. But even that verdict had brought her no real peace of mind. A part of Laurel lived in fear that someday her father would come back and hurt her again.

And then there was Matt. Matt, who had an excellent

reputation as a ladies' man. Matt, who according to the two women she'd overheard talking at a fund-raiser once, was the kind of lover who could make "the earth move." But rather than heal the injuries her father had left behind, Matt had made them bleed all over again.

Until Trent had shown her otherwise, she'd hated the very thought of lovemaking. As far as she'd been concerned, the only good that had *ever* come out of the indignities she'd suffered was Cody.

Trent was patience personified, making no demands, moving so carefully, so slowly that time had stood still for her.

If only…

It's too late. You hurt him badly once. No, twice. She realized that she'd stuck the knife into his heart by turning down his proposal, and then she'd twisted it when she'd admitted she had married someone else.

She leaned her forehead against the cooling glass, watching Trent and Cody. Twilight made it more difficult to see.

To his credit, Trent was still doing his best, working with the boy, doing far more than she'd ever expected. But there was only so much she could ask of him. His forgiveness wasn't part of that. It wouldn't be fair.

An ache built in her chest.

They looked good together, she thought. And while Cody still wasn't talking, he was definitely relating, communicating in a fashion. Cody was venturing out of his cave. For now, she had to be content with that.

She saw Trent looking her way. Laurel straightened. Trent waved, then said something to Cody. The next moment, her son waved to her, as well. A bubble of happiness rose in her chest, temporarily crushing the ache.

Ever since the trip to Knott's Berry Farm, almost a month ago, Trent had made a point of involving Cody in interactive events. Friday night had become a "family night" of sorts. Trent would bring over board games for them to play and upbeat, cheerful family-oriented movies that they all watched together.

And after the games or the movie was over, he would put Cody to bed and read to him. But first he always gave the boy the option of reading to him instead. Cody never did, but that didn't keep Trent from making the suggestion the following week.

Laurel had started reading stories to Cody the other six nights when she put him to bed.

Friday night was also the night that Trent would stay over. It hadn't initially begun that way, but after Cody had fallen asleep, within the dormant house things would heat up between them and they would wind up making love.

The first time that had happened, when he had begun to get up from her bed to go home, she'd placed her hand on his arm and quietly asked him to stay.

Moved, unable to say no to her, Trent had slipped back into bed and made love to her as if he'd never done it before. After that, she hadn't had to ask, he just remained, always taking care to be up, dressed and on his way home before Cody got up Saturday morning.

Laurel sighed again. They were playing house, she thought. And, God help her, she was content to let things go on indefinitely, even though she knew in her heart that they really couldn't. Someday, if Trent was successful, if he finally found a way to free Cody of his self-imposed prison, there would be no reason anymore for him to come over. No more reason to bring the books and the videos and the inventive games. His work would be done.

She had no illusions about what was going on between her and Trent. Two people could be together without it ever culminating in marriage. It happened all the time. She'd missed her opportunity and that was that. And if marriage was what she wanted, she knew without being told that she would be sorely disappointed.

It just wasn't going to happen.

For now, she told herself, watching Trent remove the hot dog from Cody's skewer and place it on a bun for the him, all she wanted was for this to go on a little while longer. Yes, she'd garnered more happiness than she'd ever thought possible, but she wanted just a little more time to savor Trent and his interaction with her son.

Please, God, she silently prayed. *Just a little longer.*

Letting the drape fall back into place, Laurel quietly retreated from the window.

"So, how's it going?"

Trent stopped typing and looked up from the keyboard. After all these years, a light Irish lilt still clung to Kate's voice, hinting that she was in this country by choice, not by an accident of birth.

Kate stood in his doorway, smiling at him. The man he was merged with the child he'd been and both responded to her with infinite fondness.

"Okay," he answered.

It was a vague answer aimed at life in general. He was consumed with trying to bring about another breakthrough for Cody. He abruptly remembered that he'd skipped the last couple of family get-togethers. Kate wasn't the type to subtly attempt to make him feel guilty—which was exactly why he suddenly felt guilty. Kate asked for very little.

As if reading his thoughts, she settled the matter for him. "I'm talking about Laurel's son."

He raised his brow in surprise. "How did you know I was still treating him?" Cody's treatment was completely off the books. And then, as Kate smiled, he remembered that Kelsey was still tutoring the boy, although less and less since he was doing a great deal better at school now. "Oh. I forgot. Kelsey." Kate gave a small, almost imperceptible nod of her head. "No offense, Mom, but Kelsey could talk the ears off an elephant."

The comment made her laugh. "We all have our strengths, Trent." And then, slowly, her smile grew serious. "Are you making any more progress with him?" She knew the boy still wasn't talking because Kelsey would have mentioned a breakthrough.

"Some," he allowed, if you counted eye contact and

smiles, he thought. "I've got him to the point where he's making sounds."

Getting through to a young patient could be frustrating, but Trent was a born natural with an endless supply of patience. "But not words," Kate guessed.

"No, not words," he confirmed. "I keep thinking I'm on the edge of a breakthrough and then—" he shrugged "—it doesn't happen."

"If anyone can do it, you can," Kate told him, patting his shoulder. "And how are things with Laurel?"

It was a loaded question. If anyone else besides Kate had asked it, he would have been on his guard. "What kind of things?"

"Personal things." She watched Trent lift his shoulders and then drop them in a wordless shrug. When he said nothing, she continued. "I'm not going to tell you the obvious, Trent—that you're too close to this." She saw him open his mouth and she clarified her point. "I'm not going to tell you the obvious because, to be honest, in your shoes, I would probably be doing the same thing. But I am worried about you getting hurt again," she confided, lightly brushing her fingers along his hair.

He smiled, thinking how lucky he and his brothers were that his father had met Kate.

"Is that the psychologist in you talking?"

"No, that's the mother in me talking," Kate acknowledged. "No matter what happens, I will *always* be your mother first."

He knew that, but sometimes it was nice to hear her say it out loud. He patted her hand and nodded.

"I know."

She needed to get back to her office. She had a patient coming in a few minutes. "Listen, since you're spending more and more time with them in your off-hours, why don't the three of you come over for dinner this Sunday?"

He was afraid that would be too confining for Laurel. He tried his best not to make strides with just Cody, but with her as well. Yes, they were making love, something that hadn't happened in college, but a part of him kept expecting her to take off again if he made the wrong move. It was like trying to tame a wild doe that had seen more than her share of hunters. He had to be alert.

"We're not a set, Kate."

Kate caught the change immediately. He had called her Kate, not Mom. "I didn't say you were," she replied easily. "If you recall, when you lived at home, I used to invite your friends over."

Yes, she did. And there had been times, when his brothers and Kelsey all brought people over, that the table had become a mob scene. Until Kate had taken charge. She'd always had a way about her that would make *anyone* listen to her.

Amusement erased his frown. "Is that what you're doing? Inviting my friends?"

She eyed him for a long moment. "I'm doing whatever it takes to make my son realize that he's not alone in this. That we support him no matter what he does—or whatever happens."

He remembered how, when Laurel had turned him

down and then switched colleges, in effect disappearing out of his life, he'd felt as if he were coming apart. All the abandonment issues he'd suffered when his mother had died in the plane accident had surfaced again with a vengeance. For a while, no one could talk to him, no one could get through. Not his father, not his brothers. Not Kelsey.

Only Kate.

Just like the first time, it was Kate who had made a small hole in the wall of his prison, and then another, and another until the barriers came down.

"I know that, Mom. And I appreciate it, but there's nothing to worry about. Really."

"Good," she responded cheerfully. Worry was a mother's prerogative. But she couldn't live his life for him, couldn't spin a barrier of Bubble Wrap around him to keep him safe. That wouldn't be fair. "But a little reinforcement can't hurt." Rounding his desk, she leaned over and kissed the top of his head. "Now, if you don't mind, I need you to cover Bailey's four-o'clock patient for me."

Bailey Anderson had been with the firm a year longer than he had. He was an amiable enough man, but they rarely socialized on or off the job. "Where's Bailey?"

"I had to send him home," Kate told him. "I guess the walls are thicker than I thought. He's been sneezing all morning long. He's a walking case of the flu." Her eyes searched his face. "Can you do it? I already checked your schedule and you're free. Lucas isn't," she added, mentioning the other psychologist. "I realize that it's Friday, but

I'd really take this as a favor. I'd do it myself, but I have a family consult."

No, he thought, he wasn't free, even though there was no name written in his schedule for four o'clock. It was Friday and he purposely didn't see patients after three. That way he could beat out the Friday homeward-bound traffic in order to see Laurel and Cody.

But Kate rarely asked him for a favor and he hated saying no to her. So after a beat he nodded.

"Sure, I can take over in a pinch. Just tell Rita to send the patient over to my office when he gets here. It is a he, isn't it?"

She nodded. "It's a he. And I've already told Rita that you're taking over." She placed a folder on his desk. "I thought you might like to glance through this before he comes in."

He looked at her, bemused. "I take it you assumed I'd say yes?"

Kate smiled. She paused to cup his cheek affectionately before leaving. "You were always a very good kid."

A string of ex-nannies somewhere had a very different opinion of him, as well as his brothers. "Even when I almost toppled the mannequin onto that saleswoman in Sears?"

He referred to one of a string of misadventures that had taken place when she had first come to take care of him and his brothers. She'd barely had time to push the woman out of harm's way. Trent had been very contrite and had expected to be punished. She'd done neither, which had impressed him so much he had tried his level best to be good. Or as good as someone filled with mischief could be.

"Even then," she assured him. Just before walking out the door, she said, "Don't forget to call Laurel to tell her you'll be late."

Trent's mouth dropped open. "How did you…?"

She didn't bother turning around as she answered the half-formed question. "I'm your mother. I know everything."

Though he didn't see her face, he knew she was grinning. He also knew that she was right.

Chapter Thirteen

Progress with Cody had come to a standstill. And it bothered Trent to no end.

Granted, they hadn't slid backward in the last three weeks, which was rewarding in itself.

But he wanted more.

Because of Kate, Trent had gone into his chosen profession with no illusions. He wasn't expecting earth-shaking breakthroughs from the prescribed therapy time. He knew that working with children in this field required even more patience than usual, that progress was made in tiny increments spread out over the sands of time.

But a part of him was his father's son. A part of him was goal oriented, steadily keeping his eye on the prize, and in this case the prize was the formation of a word, *any* word that would voluntarily emerge from the boy's lips. Cody seemed happier than when he'd begun this process.

But still…

It drove him crazy.

If he had to be honest, Trent knew he was too close. That was why he was doing it off the books. Because he wanted to help and because he cared. He silently argued that because he cared, he'd been allotted an extra dose of patience another psychologist might be lacking. But now that argument wore thin.

Everything was frozen in its present state with no sign of further movement. Cody made eye contact. Cody responded. Cody even smiled. He rarely crashed the video games he played. But despite all that, Cody was still in prison, still behind a glass wall, and Trent was still stumped as to why the boy had subconsciously incarcerated himself.

Trent kept coming back to his theory that the key was the accident. Trying to work in parallel, he delved back into his own experience, his own feelings that had erupted when his mother had died.

It was still a painful experience for him despite the years that had passed. But he knew he had to go through those feelings. It might be the only way to find some overlooked avenue that he could use to reach Cody, an avenue that Laurel's son was still on.

He voiced his thoughts out loud as he and Kate sat in his office, sharing a take-out lunch.

His stepmother listened quietly, treating him like a colleague rather than her son. When he finished, she made a suggestion that she knew he would rather not hear. But she would be doing him a disservice if she didn't at least put it out there.

"Maybe you should turn over the case to someone else, Trent. Someone who might be more impartial. A fresh set of eyes."

Trent shook his head. "I can't," he protested with feeling. "I can't just quit."

"It isn't quitting," she pointed out. "It's using good judgment. If he wasn't Laurel's son and you'd hit this impasse…" She deliberately allowed her voice to trail off, leaving it up to him to fill in what was left unsaid.

Yes, it mattered that Cody was Laurel's son. But for a trick of fate, he could have been his son, as well. But ultimately, it didn't change the way he felt about the matter. Committed. He hadn't signed on for just the easy cases, he'd signed on to help no matter how difficult the problem.

"I'd still try to find a way," he told her.

Kate believed him. At times, she forgot how noble he could be. "All right, then, find a way," she said. "Keep chipping away at the problem until you find an opening."

He was trying hard, but he was running out of angles and was open to any suggestions. Twenty-some-odd years ago, Kate had willingly walked into the quagmire, taking on not just one, but all of them, four themes and variations of Cody.

"You had four of us to deal with when you first came to live with us. Four kids in various stages of being shut down because of the hurt they felt. How did you cope with that?"

"I prayed a lot," she quipped. "And I loved you—all of you." Finished eating, she cleared her sandwich wrapping off his desk. "And I had puppets," she added with a wink.

The puppets were fun, but that wasn't what he remembered about the beginning. "And a great deal of patience."

"That, too." Tossing the wrapper into his wastepaper basket, she rose, dusting off her hands before she patted his shoulder. Kate was concerned, but she knew better than to interfere and overstep her bounds. Everyone needed to find their own way. The lessons learned made a deeper impression that way. She paused, looking into his eyes. "You know where to find me if you need to talk. Or to bounce off ideas."

Trent stared at the door long after she'd closed it behind her.

Yes, he knew where to find her if he needed her. Moreover, just knowing that Kate was available to him, night or day, was a great comfort. While he was close to his brothers and father, and even Kelsey, Kate was the unifying factor in his life.

In all their lives.

Unconsciously, he supposed that was what he'd been trying to give to Cody. By coming over and having the sessions at the boy's home, by taking out not just the boy but his mother to places like the amusement park, or to his parents' home as he had last week, he'd been trying to give Cody someone he could count on. Someone he could turn to.

For some reason, that someone wasn't Laurel right now. If it had been, Cody would have come out of his shell.

Casting about for some solution, Trent had decided that Cody needed a male role model in his life. Not to replace his father but to give him another authority figure to turn to.

But that had only gone so far. Another standstill.

Maybe he needed more information about what had happened that day in order to get to the root of the problem.

"The exact date that Matt was killed?" Laurel echoed Trent's question later that evening when he'd come over for the usual session. She watched him, confused.

"And the exact location as well," he added.

They hadn't touched on this since the first week. Revisiting all that made her uncomfortable. She wanted that day to remain in her past. "Why do you want to know?"

"I'm trying to pull together as much information as possible about what happened," he told her. "There has to be something I'm missing."

"Beyond the trauma of a little boy finding himself trapped in a car with the lifeless body of the father he loved?" He had all the information, she thought. Why pick at a scab? Why not just leave it alone and let it heal?

"Beyond that," he said matter-of-factly. "What happened to Cody isn't as unusual as you might think. Car accidents are all too common, and in a lot of cases someone inside the vehicle dies while someone else lives. Those survivors don't all go mute."

That was a generality. This was a specific case. She didn't see how any of what he was asking would help, but she knew better than to leave a stone unturned. She'd drive herself crazy wondering if perhaps that would have provided a solution.

In addition, she felt guilty. Guilty that she looked forward to interludes with Trent despite the fact that her son was still suffering, still trapped.

"March sixteenth of last year," she told Trent. She could still remember that awful phone call, asking her to come to the hospital. Asking her to come to the morgue to identify the body of her husband. "One day before St. Patrick's Day. The accident happened at ten-thirty in the morning on Pacific Coast Highway just past Laguna Beach." She banked down a queasy feeling over the idea that Cody could have been killed, too. "Anything else?"

He had one more question. "Who was the first responder to come on the scene?"

She paused for a moment, trying to remember what she'd been told—or even if she'd been told. "Paramedics, I think. Maybe the police." And then she shrugged. She'd been too shaken up to remember the events clearly. "I wasn't there." Her voice broke.

He immediately felt guilty. "I'm sorry, Laurel, I don't mean to make you go through this again."

She waved away his apology. This was for Cody. If he had an idea of how to reach him, he needed to follow it through.

"Do what you have to do. Just help him."

"I will," he promised, knowing he had no right to make

a guarantee. Knowing he couldn't come out and qualify his words to Laurel. If ever anyone needed to hang on to the promise of a miracle, it was Laurel.

And he intended to move heaven and earth to get it for her.

It took him a while before he managed to track down the report that gave the exact license number of the paramedics' ambulance. The company was called Immediate Response, but the vehicle in question was now being driven by two other paramedics. The pair who'd responded on March sixteenth last year, he discovered, no longer worked for the company. One of the paramedics had transferred to Albuquerque to be closer to his wife's family, and the other had retired at the beginning of the year.

Trent went to see the latter in person.

Evan Hodges was a pleasant man of average height and weight who didn't look as if he were actually old enough to retire. He looked pleased when Trent made the observation.

"Put in twenty-two years," Hodges volunteered proudly.

They were sitting outside, beneath the man's patio, overlooking a small expanse of freshly mowed grass. Not a single thing was out of place in the yard. Time apparently hung heavily on the man's hands, Trent thought.

Hodges leaned in closer so that his voice wouldn't carry beyond his guest.

"Might have put in another twenty-two, but my wife, she

wants to travel around before we have to do it in wheelchairs." The dismissive shrug told Trent that travel really held no appeal for the man. "So I said okay. But I miss working," he confided. For a moment as he spoke, his eyes shone. "It was hectic but good. Got the old blood pumping. And saving a life, hell, there's just nothing like it, you know?"

Trent nodded. "Not firsthand," he admitted, "but I can imagine." When he'd introduced himself he'd already explained to Hodges why he'd sought him out. Hungry for interaction with someone other than his wife, the man had pulled him inside and presented him with a frosty glass of lemonade before agreeing to answer his questions. "Do you remember anything at all about that incident?"

Hodges shook his head. "Can't say that I do. Except for feeling sorry for the little kid." Genuine pity infiltrated his features. "Poor kid, he didn't know his father was dead until he overheard Randy—that was my partner—good man but he never knew when to stop talking. Anyway, the kid didn't know his father was dead until he overheard Randy tell the cop on the scene."

"How did you know he didn't know?"

Hodges took a long sip of his lemonade before answering. "'Cause he got all quiet—"

"Wait," Trent interrupted. "Cody was talking until then?"

"Yeah." Hodges looked at him as if to say he should have realized that. "The kid was the one who called nine-one-one. Smart little kid. Probably saved his own life by doing it." Hodges shivered, remembering. "The car caught fire just as we got his father's body out of it."

Trent still had his doubts. "You sure he was the one who called nine-one-one?"

In response, Hodges raised his sloping shoulders and let them drop again in a careless shrug. "That's what they told me."

Trent was on his feet instantly. "Thanks," he told the former paramedic, shaking his hand with feeling. "Thanks very much. I know my way out," Trent assured him, going through the gate that led out to the front of the house.

"Did I help?" the man asked, calling after him.

"You helped a lot," Trent assured him before closing the gate behind him.

It took some doing. In the end, he had to resort to having Travis, who knew people on the police force, pull some strings for him. But he did manage to listen to the tape of the 911 call from the accident that claimed the life of Cody's father.

The dispatcher, a dark-skinned woman closer to twenty than thirty, was only too happy to take a break in her day and play the tape for him.

"Got it for you right here," she told him. "You must know some pretty important people to get this kind of treatment," she marveled, preparing to play the tape for him.

"Not me, my brother." Somewhere along the line, there had even been a police detective or two involved. But all he cared about was hearing the tape.

Obligingly, the dispatcher played it for him. "There's not much," she warned.

A childish, frightened voice crackled on the tape the minute the dispatcher came on the line.

"My daddy's sleeping and he won't wake up. The car crashed. Please come and help him."

The dispatcher asked Cody a series of questions and he answered as best he could, growing progressively more agitated and begging for her to come help his father. And then the line went dead.

"That's all there is," the woman said.

A cold shiver ran down Trent's spine. Cody had talked. He had still been able to talk at that point. What had changed between then and when he had been extracted from the mangled vehicle?

"Can I get a copy of that?" he asked, nodding at the tape.

The young woman frowned slightly. "We don't generally give out copies," she began.

"The little boy on the tape doesn't talk anymore," Trent told her, showing her a picture of Cody. "There's nothing physically wrong with him. It's all traumatic and I'm trying to get him to come around."

She handed back the picture, clearly moved. "And listening to the nine-one-one call he made on the worst day of his life is going to make him talk?"

Trent slipped the photograph back into his pocket. "You never know what's going to work. Everything else I've tried hasn't."

The dispatcher debated for a moment, then gave in.

"All right," she said. "Let me see what I can do." Rather than go through the chain of command, she quickly made a copy on a CD and handed it to him. "It didn't come from me," she told him.

"What didn't?" he asked, pocketing the mini-CD.

The woman flashed him a blinding smile just before he turned and walked away.

Trent weighed all the possible pros and cons of the situation, trying to second-guess any repercussions that might occur if Cody listened to the tape. Mainly, he focused on all the things that could go wrong.

First and foremost, it could blow up in his face and he could lose all the progress he'd made so far. But since that progress was incomplete, it could be viewed as minor in the scheme of things. And if playing the CD won back the boy, then maybe it would be worth the risk.

A nagging little voice warned that it wasn't his risk to take, but he ignored it. For Cody's sake.

Trent said nothing to Laurel about what he planned to do when he came over the next evening. She didn't press him beyond asking if he'd had any luck tracking down the paramedics. He told her the truth, that one had left the state and the other had retired.

Because he said nothing further, she left it at that, assuming he hadn't spoken to either man. She gestured toward the rear of the house. "Cody's in the family room, as usual." She smiled, her hands clasped before her hopefully. "I think he's actually waiting for you."

Trent murmured, "That's good," before heading for the family room.

The door was ajar. He knocked, then entered. When he greeted the boy, Cody looked up in his direction before resuming his game. Next to him on the rug was the second control pad, an unspoken invitation to join him in the video game. It was the same unspoken invitation he'd issued for a month now.

Trent slid into place beside the boy on the floor. "You remember I told you that my mom died when I was about the same age as you?" Cody inclined his head slightly, indicating that he remembered. "And that I felt guilty because I thought that maybe, if I'd been a better boy, if I hadn't fought with my brothers, or answered her back, she wouldn't have wanted to go on a trip without me, without us, and she wouldn't have died. I thought it was my fault she died. I thought that for a long time.

"But it wasn't my fault. It wasn't anyone's fault. It was just something that happened," he told Cody without bothering to censor his emotions. "Your dad wouldn't have wanted you to be like this. He would have wanted you to move on, to be good to your mom and be happy."

He noted that Cody pressed the control pad harder. The movements on the screen were faster, jerkier.

Hesitating for a second, Trent took the small CD player out of his pocket and pressed Play.

Cody stiffened the moment he heard his own voice. The boy's eyes grew large as he eyed him accusingly. And then he swung his hand out, sending the CD player flying out of Trent's hand and onto the tile floor. The sound stopped the second the CD player made contact with the ceramic tiles, breaking.

Trent ignored the broken player, concentrating instead on the broken boy.

"It's not your fault, Cody. I know you probably think it is, but it's not. You did everything you could to help. You even called nine-one-one. Most kids your age wouldn't have done that. And a lot of adults wouldn't have had the presence of mind to call, either. The paramedics tried to save your dad, but he was already dead when they got there. Nobody could have helped," he emphasized, then repeated again, "It wasn't your fault, Cody."

Tears streamed down the small, oval face. And then, in a lost, hoarse voice, the words, "Yes, it is," echoed through the room. "I killed him. I killed my dad," Cody cried.

For a moment, Trent focused not on the words, but the fact that there were any words at all.

He'd done it. He'd broken through to the boy.

Trying not to act as if this were anything out of the ordinary, as if this were nothing more than a conversation between him and any other child he'd been treating, Trent asked in an even tone, "Why would you say that?"

"Because he was mad at me," Cody sobbed. "Because I said something and he was looking at me when the truck came."

Trent was aware of exactly the way the events had transpired, thanks to the police report. Pacific Coast Highway, narrow and winding in places with more than its share of blind spots, was a difficult road to navigate at times. A truck had come around from behind a blind spot and, since he wasn't paying strict attention to the road, Cody's father had clipped the truck and sent his own car spinning out of control. The sedan had landed upside down and trapped its two occupants.

"It's all my fault," Cody cried again, sobbing bitterly.

Abandoning protocol, going with his gut instincts, Trent took the little boy into his arms and held him as he cried his heart out.

He held on to Cody for a long time.

Chapter Fourteen

An antsy feeling danced through Laurel as she made her way from the kitchen to the family room. She carried a tray piled high with chocolate chip cookies still warm from the oven. The scent wrapped around and drifted behind her like the tail of a kite soaring through the air, but she was only marginally aware of it.

She struggled to harness her thoughts and get them under control. The last thing she wanted was for her agitation to show. It might disrupt Cody and she knew that Trent would ask her about it.

Laurel didn't want to talk.

At the same time, she wanted to tap into the positive energy that Trent could generate just by being here. He'd told her more than once that he was trying to keep his sessions with Cody informal and relaxed. She didn't think that either one of them would mind having a cookie break and it would provide her an excuse to be with them, at least for a few minutes.

Maybe a few minutes with them was all she needed to calm this restlessness within her, this feeling of not knowing where to turn, what to do.

She'd come so far, worked so hard to rise above everything, and yet, here it was, back again. That awful feeling that had all but smothered her as a child. And all because her mother had given her a letter.

She was told it had arrived a week ago. Although it had been sent care of her mother's house, it was addressed to her.

It was a letter from her father. The man she'd convinced herself was dead.

Grace Valentine had spent an entire week trying to decide whether or not to give her daughter the letter, silently arguing with herself.

"I was going to just throw it away," she'd finally told her when she'd come over this morning. "You've suffered enough because of him. But then I thought that I had no right to do that. That you could decide for yourself if you wanted to read it or destroy it. I even debated opening it and reading it myself so I could decide whether or not it would hurt you to see it," her mother had confessed.

Her mouth had curved in that sad smile that was so typical of her. "A mother's protective instincts are very strong, my love. But you're a grown woman," she'd gone on to say, "and capable of making your own decisions."

Opening her purse, she'd taken out the long, slender envelope and placed it on the table between them. "So here, here's his letter." She snapped her purse closed again. The sound seemed to echo along the vaulted ceilings. "You decide what you want to do with it."

She'd left soon afterward.

And just like that, the man who had nearly destroyed her life was back in it. In spirit if not in body, which somehow made it a great deal worse. She could have slammed the door on him if he'd been on her doorstep. This missive haunted her as she tried to go about her morning as if nothing had happened.

So far, she hadn't opened it. And she had fished it out of the trash three times. Which, as far as she could see, made her a prisoner not just of indecision, but of her father as well.

She hadn't said anything to Trent about the letter, because she didn't want him to know that thoughts of dealing with her father could still make her break out in a cold sweat. Besides, she didn't want anything distracting him from working with Cody. Except for maybe, momentarily, chocolate chip cookies.

With a toss of her head, Laurel willed a smile onto her lips and walked into the family room.

She took one step across the threshold before stopping. One step before she realized that she wasn't listening to the sound of Trent's voice, nor to the sound from the large-screen TV that Cody used for his games.

The small, childlike voice she heard belonged to Cody.

The tray slipped from her lax fingers, hitting the

carpeted floor with a jarring noise. The pile of cookies rose into the air, then fell, dispersing along the tray. Only a couple wound up on the floor.

Trent was on his feet and beside her in a flash. "Are you all right?" he asked, concerned.

She'd looked preoccupied when he'd come over today. Even when he'd spoken with her, he had a feeling she wasn't completely processing what he was saying. He'd tried to coax her into talking, but she had brushed him off with a faint smile and a denial, telling him that she was fine.

He hadn't believed it for a second, but he knew better than to press her. She'd only wind up internalizing whatever it was that bothered her, making it that much harder to decipher. He tried to tell himself that she'd turn to him when the time came. After all, hadn't they come a long way since the time when she'd just vanished on him?

He supposed that he still lived with that fear of putting his heart on the line.

"He's talking," Laurel said hoarsely, staring at Cody in wonder. Dazed, she was afraid to believe what her ears had heard. Afraid of the disappointment that would prove to be so much sharper if she was wrong. Her eyes shifted to Trent, pleading for confirmation, for reassurance. "I heard him talking."

Trent beckoned the boy over, casually slipping his arm around his thin shoulders. He acted as if this was the most normal thing in the world instead of an outstanding breakthrough.

"Of course he's talking. Cody's been talking since he

was, what, nine months old?" he asked, glancing down at Cody for confirmation, even though there was no way the boy could remember that.

In response, Cody bobbed his head up and down solemnly. "That's what Mom said. Right, Mom?" he asked, turning to her.

Laurel dropped to her knees before her son, taking hold of his shoulders, afraid that it was all a dream and that he'd vanish on her. But it wasn't a dream. He was still here. She searched his face. It was true. He was back.

"Oh Cody, I've missed the sound of your voice so much." Breaking down, she threw her arms around the boy and held him to her, her tears dampening his shoulder.

For a moment, Cody gave in and put his arms around her as best he could, taking comfort in the warmth, in the feel of being united with his mother again. And then, the part of him that was a male child striving for independence rallied, and he squirmed just a little.

"You're getting my shoulder wet, Mom."

She laughed then, rocking back on her heels and wiping away her tears with the heel of her hand.

"Sorry. Couldn't help myself." And then she beamed. "But you're talking. You're actually talking." Her attention shifted to the miracle worker she'd invited back into her life and she looked up at Trent. "How did you do it?"

Happy, at a loss how to frame her question, all words seemed to escape her.

"It was just time," Trent told her simply. And then, because he knew she needed details, he said to Cody,

"Why don't you start on the snack your mom made for us? I'd like to talk to her for a minute or two."

Why did that sound so foreboding to her? She'd just received the best news in the whole world, so why did a feeling of dread weave in and out of her?

Solemnly, the boy nodded and turned his attention to the cookies that he'd helped gather up.

Trent gently took hold of Laurel's arm and moved her over to the far side of the room, leaving Cody to happily sample what she'd baked.

"What did you say to him?" she asked. Trent's statement that it was time for Cody to start talking again was all well and good, but it didn't begin to explain what had happened, what had finally prompted Cody to abandon his world of silence. And she desperately needed to know.

"I didn't say anything. I played back his own words to him," Trent told her. "Did you know that he was the one who made the nine-one-one call to the police?"

She slowly shook her head. "No. I just assumed it was the other driver, or someone passing by the accident. I thought Cody had stopped talking when he saw that his father was dead."

"He didn't realize he was," Trent said. "According to the paramedic on the scene, Cody thought your husband was unconscious. Asleep, not dead," he clarified. "He only found out when he overheard the policeman talking to the other paramedic."

She tried to make sense out of it but was at a loss. "And that made him stop talking?"

Trent turned his back to Cody so that the boy couldn't make out his words. "No, guilt did."

What kind of guilt could a five-year-old boy have? "Guilt?"

Trent nodded. "He told me that your husband was angry with him, that Matt was reprimanding him for something and not paying attention to the road when the truck came around the bend. Cody said he screamed out a warning and Matt tried to avoid hitting the truck at the last moment. You know the rest."

She was still somewhat confused. "You said you played his own words for him?"

"I got a copy of the nine-one-one call he made. I thought that maybe if I jarred him a little, if I had him relive the event to an extent, I could get to the root of what made him stop talking."

The 911 call. She hadn't even thought of that. "How did you manage to get the tape?"

He shrugged carelessly. "I pulled a couple of strings, or had Travis do it. He knows a few people on the police force."

And he'd done all that, gone through all that trouble, for her. For Cody, which was like doing it for her. "I don't know how to thank you." How many times had she said this to him in the last two months? It seemed so paltry as repayment.

He stopped her right there. He knew that people had a tendency to think that once a breakthrough was reached, that was the end of it. But it wasn't. It was just the beginning.

"It's not over yet, Laurel," he warned her. "Just because Cody's talking doesn't mean that he's out of the woods. He's going to need some more therapy for a while to help him deal with his feelings of guilt."

Guilt. The boy had nothing to feel guilty about. It was an accident, pure and simple. But Trent was the expert here, so she'd go along with what he thought was best.

"Well, fine then. You do what you have to do."

Instead of agreeing, she was surprised to see Trent shake his head. "No, I think he might be better off if someone else saw him now."

Her nerves were tight.

"Why not you?"

"Because I'm too close." Kate had been right. He needed to turn this over to someone else. He'd made the breakthrough, now it was time for a fresh perspective. "I told myself before that caring about Cody could only help him in the long run, but at this point I think he'd be better off with someone more impartial."

All she could think of was that Cody would start to backslide again. Cody needed Trent in his life. And God help her, so did she.

Was this payback? she wondered suddenly. Was Trent stepping back, walking away because she'd done the same thing to him?

"He won't talk to anyone else," she heard herself saying, her voice echoing in her head.

Trent smiled as he shook his head. He glanced back at Cody for a second. "I think you need to give him a little more credit than that," he told her. "He's a brave, strong boy, capable of getting through this."

The hurt she felt was incredible. She could barely breathe. Her only thought was that Trent was leaving her. Leaving them. "So you're just going to hand him over to someone else?"

She looked pale, he thought. Why? "Not just 'someone else,'" he assured her. "I have someone in mind. There're a couple of other psychologists in our office who could step in." He hesitated mentioning Kate because she was, after all, family, and the idea was to have someone outside the circle take over now. "They're both fine, caring people."

"But not you."

"No, not me." Didn't she understand that he was doing it for Cody? That now that there'd been this breakthrough, progress could be better achieved if someone else handled it? Besides, he had a different role in mind for himself.

How could she feel so awful after something so wonderful had happened? Her son was talking. He'd finally come out of his trance, his coma, his self-imposed death sentence, to rejoin the living. She should be overjoyed.

Instead, she felt abandoned. Left stranded on some ice floe in the Antarctic. Trent was leaving her, just as she'd once left him.

She wanted to plead with him, to ask him why he was doing this. She wanted to beg him to stay.

But even as she thought that, Laurel knew in her heart that she didn't want him on those terms. She only wanted him if he wanted her. If *he* wanted to remain, not go.

"I see," she murmured. "All right, I'll have him see whomever you think is best for him." She turned her eyes to his face. "I guess we won't be seeing you anymore, then."

There was an odd expression on her face, he noted. Was that what she thought? That he was trying to disengage from them? Or was that what she wanted? "Not professionally," he said cautiously.

He watched her mouth curve with a bitter smile. "Was that all this was? Just professional? Might make an interesting article, treating mother and son at the same time. Bringing them both back around. Guess that probably puts you in the running for psychologist of the year."

Trent watched her, stunned. What in God's name was she talking about? "Laurel, what's wrong?"

"Wrong?" she echoed. "Nothing's wrong," she declared, barely holding back her anger, her hurt. She struggled to keep her voice down so that Cody couldn't hear. "What could be wrong? You gave me back my son. Showed me sex didn't have to make me feel terrible. Everything is perfect." And then she stopped abruptly, hearing the hitch in her own voice. "I'm sorry. I think I'm just a little overwhelmed here. I thought that you and I—oh, never mind." She waved her hand dismissively.

"I never liked a half-finished sentence, Laurel," he told her. "What about you and me?"

"Nothing." It was all she could do not to snap at him. "There is no 'you and me.' Don't you think I realize that? You were just trying to help me deal with my own demons. And you did. You helped a great deal and don't think I'm not grateful. I am. Very grateful." She tossed her head, sending her hair flying about her shoulders. Her mind scrambled for a plausible excuse. "It's just that I'm not used to being happy and I'm having a little trouble processing all this. But don't worry, I will."

Trent wanted to demand to know why she was pushing him out of her life again. But he'd been on this route with her before, going from elation to confusion, to indescribable hurt. He had absolutely no desire to be on the receiving end of something like that again.

At the very least, they needed some space between them. "Look, maybe I'd better leave."

"All right," she replied stiffly, even as her heart broke in half. "If that's what you want."

No, that wasn't what he wanted. But there was something happening here, something he needed time to understand. "I'll call you with the name of a good child psychologist."

"Great." She nodded, suddenly feeling restless again. "I'm sure that whoever you pick will be very good." Not as excellent as him, but then, who was?

Damn it, she couldn't think like that. If she did, she was going to fall apart.

"Just let me say good-night to Cody," he said, retracing his steps to the boy.

She almost said, "Don't you mean goodbye?" but she bit back the words because Cody had to be protected at all costs. Even if he hadn't started talking again, Cody was very attached to Trent.

They both were.

Cody looked confused. "You're going away?"

"No, not away. I just have to leave right now." Needing an excuse, he had said the first thing that had come into his mind. "I have another patient who needs me tonight."

"Just like me?" Cody asked.

"No one is just like you," Trent told him with affection. "But close, yes."

Cody seemed sad at the prospect of his leaving, but he nodded his head. "Okay. But I'll miss you," he said out of the blue.

Makes two of us, champ, Trent thought as he ruffled the boy's hair.

"I'll be right back," Laurel promised Cody. "I'm just going to walk Dr. Trent to the door."

Turning away from the family room, she walked in front of Trent, trying not to think. Trying to pretend that he was just another person passing through her life and not, as she'd come to briefly believe, her soul mate.

She was to blame for everything, not him. With great effort, she forced a smile to her lips. "Again, thank you very much for what you've done." Then, before she broke down in front of him, she quickly shut the door, then leaned her head against it, willing herself to go numb. She wouldn't have been able to bear it any other way.

Trent didn't even know how he found himself on the other side of the door. One minute she was talking to him and he was debating asking her what was wrong one more time, the next, he found himself staring at beveled glass.

The way he saw it, he had two choices. He could either make a scene and demand to be readmitted, or he could just accept the fact that he had done something special for her son and move on. If Cody overheard them arguing, it could undo his progress. Trent couldn't risk that for his own personal satisfaction.

So, with a suppressed sigh, he turned on his heel and walked away.

Laurel watched his shadow recede through the prism-like glass on the upper portion of the door. For a moment, she fought the very real urge to yank the door open again, babbling apologies, pleading temporary insanity or whatever it took to get Trent to come back in.

But she knew it was better this way. A clean break as opposed to a lingering one. That he would leave was a given. She'd hurt his pride twice over and couldn't expect that to just fade from existence.

Squaring her shoulders, Laurel turned around and walked on rubbery legs back to the family room, as large a smile as she could manage pasted on her face.

She prayed that Cody wasn't insightful or intuitive the way some intelligent children could be. She didn't want him seeing past her smile, into her heart, to the ache that was there. No, this moment was going to be all about him, she insisted silently. She'd waited a year for this to happen, for him to speak again. Now he was better and it was all that mattered.

Cody was all that mattered.

When she walked in, she saw that the boy wasn't

playing his game. He'd finished picking up the tray of cookies and had placed it neatly on the coffee table. His blue eyes raised to hers the moment she crossed the threshold.

She flashed her smile at him.

"Okay, Cody, start talking," she instructed cheerfully. "We've got a year to catch up on."

Cody's smile was almost shy. It went straight to her heart and almost erased the pain she felt.

Almost.

Chapter Fifteen

Trent stared at the rectangular piece of paper he held between his fingers. He'd been peering at it since Rita had dropped the envelope on his desk a few minutes ago. It was a check, written for an obscene amount of money.

A check.

Laurel had written him a check.

"For services rendered," the note on the bottom-left corner of the check read. She was paying him for helping Cody. Paying him as if they'd had nothing but a working, professional relationship.

As if they meant nothing to each other, beyond therapist and mother of a patient. Which made the time they'd spent together in each other's arms feel tainted, unsavory.

Instead of good and special, the way it had felt at the time.

He hadn't heard from Laurel in a week, giving her space even when he wanted nothing more than to show up at her door and reclaim what had been building so steadily between them.

"Damn it."

For some reason, the words, uttered more loudly than he'd meant, summoned Rita to his doorway. Apparently his administrative assistant had guessed at the envelope's contents.

She gave the impression that she'd been hovering in the vicinity of his office, waiting for some signal that he'd opened the envelope.

"I'm heading out to the bank," she told him as if this were a new venture rather than something she did every Wednesday and Friday morning. Rita nodded at the paper he held. "Want me to deposit that along with the other checks?"

For once, she didn't stride into the room as if she owned every square foot. Instead, she stood in the doorway, waiting for an answer. Maybe after all this time, a vein of sensitivity had finally opened up within the woman, Trent thought.

"No," he answered. "I'm going to take care of this myself."

Small, bony shoulders rose and fell in the blink of an eye. "Suit yourself. I'll leave a deposit slip on my desk for you," she offered.

Looking at the check again, he felt his jaw harden. "No need."

Rita frowned. It was obvious that she was biting her

tongue, trying not to say anything. "You did it pro bono, didn't you?" she challenged. "That's just for lawyers, you know."

Ordinarily, the eccentric assistant amused him. But he wasn't in the mood today. "Go to the bank, Rita," he instructed.

She seemed annoyed, but let it pass without further comment. "Fine. Want me to send in your first patient, or do you want a little downtime to seethe first?"

Trent glanced at his desk calendar. Every line was filled in. He had a full day ahead of him. Unless he canceled someone's session, there would be no opportunity to deal with this until after five.

His sense of obligation won out. "Send in the patient," he told her.

Rita's version of a smug smile slipped across her painfully thin lips. "Whatever you say."

That'll be the day, Trent thought. The woman marched to her own drummer, but she got the job done. Besides, they all felt that if Rita no longer had an office to come to, she would undoubtedly whither away and die.

About to leave, Rita turned her head to look at him over her shoulder. "By the way, she called me, you know."

Trent narrowed his eyes, momentarily lost in thought. "Who called you?"

A touch of impatience danced along her shallow cheeks. "Mrs. Greer. She wanted to know what you charged by the hour." She pointed toward the check. "That should be for the right amount."

It probably was, even though he hadn't counted the hours. But Laurel obviously had. Everything by the book. As if they were strangers instead of lovers with a history.

He continued staring at the check after Rita had left. Part of him thought he should just accept the payment and move on.

But the other part, the part that had never played by all the guidelines, just couldn't do that. He needed to have some questions answered before he put any of this behind him.

And then the door opened and he was a psychologist again.

"Hello, Howie," he said, greeting his twelve-year-old patient cheerfully. "So how was your week?"

Trent rang the doorbell three times before he received any sort of a response. He'd debated leaving and coming back later. The silent debate was still going on in his head when the door abruptly opened.

Laurel stood in the space between the doorjamb and the door itself, blocking entrance into her house with her body. "You were supposed to think I wasn't home."

"Then you should have hidden your car," he informed her.

"That's not my car. It's my mother's. She's picking Cody up for a sleepover." Her mouth curved slightly. "She's very excited to get her grandson back," Laurel told him.

Trent waited, but nothing further followed. So he finally asked, "Are you going to let me in?"

With a quick, nervous nod, she stepped back, opening the door further. Walking in, Trent looked around to make sure that Cody wasn't in the vicinity. His temper, the one he hadn't known he still had until this morning, was in danger of flaring up.

But Cody didn't seem to be in the immediate area. He followed Laurel as she led the way.

"My mother thinks you're a miracle worker," she told him once they reached the living room and she turned around to face him. "So do I," she added quietly.

He pulled the check she'd written out of his back pocket and held it up. He didn't bother hiding the annoyance in his voice.

"Is this the going price for miracles these days?" he asked.

Her eyes darted toward the check and then back at him. She raised her chin ever so slightly. "If it's not enough, I can—"

Before she could finish, he crumpled it in his hand, then tossed it on the coffee table. "I told you I wasn't charging you."

Laurel folded her hands together before her. "I didn't want you thinking I was taking advantage of our friendship."

"Is that what it was?" he demanded, a sharp edge entering his voice. "Just friendship? Funny, because I thought it was a great deal more."

"You know it was. For me," she tagged on.

"Then why this?" he gestured angrily at the crumpled check on the table. When she didn't answer, he asked, "Why are you backing away?"

"I'm not the one backing away," she insisted, distressed. "You are."

She caught him off guard with the accusation. He stared at her. "Me?"

"What else am I supposed to think?" Laurel asked. "You were turning Cody over to someone else."

Trent didn't see the connection. "To help him."

"And not to get away from me." It was an accusation, not a question.

"Did I say I was trying to get away from you?"

"Actions speak louder than words." When he looked at her blankly, she added, "You wouldn't be coming over anymore. And I understand, I really do."

"Then explain it to me, because I don't." He bit back his frustration and tapped into what he'd once thought of as an endless supply of patience, a supply that was dwindling fast. "What is it that you understand?"

She wasn't confrontational by nature. It was costing her to stand here, going toe to toe with him. But she did want him to understand. And maybe, just maybe, some small part of her hoped he would show her that her assumptions were wrong.

"That you can't forgive me for turning you down. For disappearing like that on you." Laurel forced herself not to look away as she said, "For marrying Matt."

"About that," he interjected before she could say anything more.

Uneasy, Laurel took a deep breath and then asked, "Yes?"

"I'd just like to know why."

"Why?" she echoed.

"Why did you marry him and not me?" He needed to know. Otherwise, it would haunt him to his grave. "You couldn't have thought that he'd love you more than I did—because no one could," he added with an almost fierce, unshakable certainty.

Laurel squared her shoulders like a soldier bracing for one last battle. A battle in which the results would be final and not at all pleasing. Again, she raised her chin, determined to see this through.

"Matt married me because he couldn't have me any other way and he liked the challenge of a conquest."

Trent shook his head. "I didn't ask you that. I asked you why *you* married him. Did you love him that much more than me?"

"No," she said with feeling. And then, because even though her reason was selfless, she was still ashamed of admitting it. "For the money."

One moment stretched out into two. And then more. Trent looked at her, stunned, the stark, cold answer glaring between them. "I don't believe you," he finally said in a low voice.

A lump suddenly formed in her throat. "It's true." She whispered so her voice wouldn't crack.

But he shook his head. "I couldn't have been that wrong about you," he insisted, his voice deadly still. "You're not the type to be bought."

She let out a long breath. "Everyone can be bought. Just

depends on the currency. You were bought with my tears. That's why you agreed to help Cody," she went on. "Because you hated seeing me so upset."

Had all that been calculated? He refused to believe she'd manipulated him. But then, why was she saying all this? "And you were bought with cold cash?"

"Yes."

Something within him crumbled. If he was so wrong about her, then what else had he been so wrong about? "What was it that you needed so desperately?"

Laurel looked away, not knowing how much longer she could keep this up. "I already told you—"

Rallying, Trent refused to believe the woman he'd loved all this time didn't really exist.

"There's more to it than that," he insisted. "There had to be."

"She did it for me."

They both turned in unison to see Laurel's mother standing in the doorway closest to the front door. Embroiled, they'd both forgotten she was still in the house.

Laurel's eyes widened in dismay. "You said you were leaving."

"I am. But Cody's still packing his toys. He's not taking his video games," she added proudly. Her eyes shifted toward Trent. Her smile was warm. It was obvious that she felt she had him to thank for that. "Nice to see you again, Trent. And thank you for giving me my grandson back."

Compliments always made Trent feel uncomfortable. He focused on what Laurel's mother had said just before she'd walked in. "What do you mean Laurel did it for you?"

If he knew, it would only make it seem worse somehow. "Mother, don't," Laurel warned.

"I needed a triple bypass and there was no insurance and no money to cover it. Matt was a billionaire who was used to getting what he wanted and he wanted Laurel. Laurel said they'd have to get married before she slept with him. He was fine with it as long as she signed a prenup that cut her off without a cent if she dissolved the marriage, and left the settlement up to him if he decided to call it off. I begged her not to do it, but she wouldn't listen," Grace Valentine confessed.

Stunned, Trent could only look at Laurel for a long moment. "You married him so that he would pay for your mother's operation?"

When Laurel said nothing, her mother told him, "They used to call that a marriage of convenience, although it didn't seem very convenient to me."

"I wasn't about to let you die and I couldn't raise the money any other way." The distress in Laurel's voice all but pulsated.

"Grandma," a childish voice called from the foyer. "I'm ready."

"Ah, music to my ears." Grace paused to squeeze Trent's hand. "You don't mind if I rush away. If Cody comes in here and sees you, we won't leave for a long time—I know how he feels about you—and I've got a pot roast in the oven, scheduled to come out. It's his favorite."

Trent nodded. "I understand."

"One in a million," she said, addressing the words over her shoulder at Laurel. "Thank you again," she repeated before raising her voice to respond, "Grandma's coming, Cody."

Trent waited until Laurel's mother had left the room. The ensuing silence was all but deafening. "Why didn't you tell me?" he asked her in a low voice.

He was angry. She knew he'd be angry. She had nothing left to give him but the truth. Not that it would help. "Because it was my business. Because it sounded like I sold my body for money. Like a prostitute."

What was that old saying? Trent tried to remember. "With a heart of gold."

She shook her head, avoiding his eyes. Not wanting to see firsthand what he thought of her. She could guess. "Still a prostitute."

Trent took hold of her shoulders, forcing her to look at him.

"Look, I realize that your father did a hell of a number on you, destroying your self-esteem, but what happened in that bedroom when you were ten was not your fault," he underscored. "Any more than the car accident that killed your husband was Cody's fault. Bad things happen to good people, things that they have no control over, but they—*you*—need to rise above," he insisted wholeheartedly. "You can't let it ruin your life. You saw that with Cody. Why can't you see that with yourself?"

It wasn't that she saw herself that way. She was afraid that he did. Raising her head, she searched his eyes. Looked into his soul. He wasn't condemning her, wasn't repulsed by what she'd done. Dear Lord, did he really understand?

She felt her heart racing as hope entered it. Taking a deep breath, she shared something else with him. "He wrote me, you know. My father. He wrote to me."

Trent was instantly alert. And troubled—for her. "When?"

"A few days ago. He sent the letter in care of my mother's address because he didn't know where I was." She'd finally forced herself to read it yesterday. A cold, clammy feeling had descended over her as she'd read the words. "In it, he apologized for what he'd done and he asked me to forgive him."

"And can you?"

She'd gone back and forth a hundred times since yesterday. "He's dying." She ran her tongue along her lips. "I should be able to, but—"

Trent honestly felt that she needed to let this go and put it behind her. Otherwise, she would always be a prisoner of that bedroom.

"If you forgive him, that shows that you're better than he is," he told her quietly. "And maybe you can finally move on."

Her breath was ragged as it escaped her lips. "Forgiving him isn't going to help me move on." She raised her eyes to his, knowing she was risking everything by putting this out there. Trent could still turn her down, say that they needed a breather after all this. But she didn't want to breathe without him. "Being with you is the only thing that is going to help me move on."

And then he grinned.

She could feel herself responding. Grinning like an idiot.

"Well then, I guess you just happen to be in luck," he told her, "because I really want to be with you."

It seemed too good to be true. She wanted to be sure, very sure. "You still want me even after you know everything?"

"I don't 'still' want you," he said, and her heart fell. His next words brought it back around again. "I have *always* wanted you, Laurel. Even when you weren't there. Before you, I didn't think I could love anyone, didn't think I could invest myself in anyone because I was afraid. Afraid of the pain of being left."

Her eyes misted over. How could she have been so stupid not to realize that he was the best thing that had ever happened to her? "And I left," she said gently.

"You did present one hell of a challenge," he admitted. "But no matter what I did, I couldn't get over you. Maybe because I didn't *want* to get over you. Somewhere inside with all that logic was the heart of an optimist who felt, if he believed hard enough, wanted hard enough, this dream would come true." He touched her face, caressing it. Loving her. "And you were my dream, Laurel. From the very first moment I saw you."

A smile blossomed. That was a little hard to believe. "In fourth grade?"

He wasn't about to retract his words. "What can I say? I was mature for my age."

She remembered their first encounter as if it were yesterday. She had been shy, introverted to the point that people were always teasing her. "You splashed me with water from the drinking fountain."

"Okay, I was semimature for my age," he amended, as he tucked his arms around her waist and drew her to him. "Marry me, Laurel."

Her eyes widened. She wasn't expecting this. She would be satisfied if he just wanted to remain in her life. "You really want to marry me?"

"I really, really want to marry you." He stole a quick kiss before continuing. "That was another reason I couldn't go on treating Cody. I wanted to propose to you. I want to be his dad, not his therapist." And then, in case she needed reinforcement, he said, "I love you, Laurel. I always have, I always will."

"I don't deserve you."

Her negative view of herself was going to take some work, but he was up to it. "Yeah, you do. And I deserve you. What do you say?"

Instead of answering him, she kissed him, long and hard, until her own head was spinning.

"No distractions," he told her when their lips parted. "I want an answer. Yes, or yes?"

The smile began in her eyes, filtering right down to her toes. "Those are my only two choices?"

He inclined his head, as if thinking. "Or you can say yes," he allowed.

"Then I guess I'll say yes."

"Good choice," he told her just before he kissed her.

And her heart, back on speaking terms with her, told her that it was.

Epilogue

"You know," Trent commented as he watched Laurel race past him for the umpteenth time, coming precariously close to the heavily decorated eight-foot Christmas tree that stood in the center of her living room, "I really didn't think it was possible to do a 10K run in a house—until today."

This time, as Laurel zoomed by in the opposite direction, heading for the kitchen to fetch the next covered dish, Trent grabbed her by the shoulders. Laurel moved so quickly, she nearly took him down with the force of her forward momentum. He held on tighter for both their sakes.

"Whoa," he ordered, prudently suppressing the laugh that rose in his throat. He knew it wouldn't have gone over well. "Calm down, Laurel. You're going to wear yourself out before they even get here."

Her mother, God bless her, was entertaining Cody in the family room to keep him out of the way. She was beginning to think she should have asked her to take Trent in tow as well.

Laurel attempted to shrug free, but failed. "But there's still so much to do before your family all gets here."

She still didn't get it yet, did she? "Laurel, they're not coming here for anything that you can 'do.' They're coming here to see you, to spend Christmas Eve here, because that was what you said you wanted," he reminded her.

She had to have been insane when she'd said that, Laurel thought. She was actually going to be serving dinner to a family with an award-winning chef in their ranks. What the hell had she been thinking?

Still, she'd volunteered, no, insisted, so she had to make the best of it. The *very* best of it.

"I did. I do," Laurel corrected, trying to shrug him off again. This time, she succeeded. "It's just that I want everything to be perfect and every second that you're holding on to my arms is a second I've lost."

This time, his eyes held her in place rather than his hands. "Is that the way you really see it?"

Laurel sighed. She willed herself to relax just a little before she had a complete meltdown. "You know that's not what I mean. But I do want everything to be—"

"Perfect, right, you already said that." He smiled at her, disarming her agitation. "The only thing that has to be perfect is you and you already are."

How had she gotten so lucky? "Oh God, Trent, how do you always know the right thing to say?"

He grinned. "It's a gift."

And then he raised his eyes upward. He'd trapped her in the doorway leading from the living room to the dining room. A doorway that he'd just finished decorating in an effort to remain out of Laurel's way. Recovering from being trampled was not the way he'd hoped to spend this evening.

"Mistletoe," Trent told her, as if sounding an alarm.

Her head was going in a dozen different directions at once. "What?"

Trent raised his eyes again, this time in an exaggerated fashion. She followed his gaze. "Mistletoe," he repeated.

"Oh." She stared at it, a slight frown furrowing her brow. "I don't remember putting that up."

"That's because you didn't. I did." It was the last thing Trent said before kissing her. The kiss lingered until he felt her melting into him. Only then did he draw his lips away. "Better?"

"Better." The word came out in a sigh. "But I still have to—"

"Come with me." He didn't let her finish. Instead, he suddenly took her by the hand and led her over to the tree. "Notice anything?" he asked her.

She stared blankly at the tree that had taken Trent, Cody and her over five hours to decorate. It shimmered and glittered beneath tons of tinsel and ropes of silver garland, as well as too many ornaments to count.

"You put on more tinsel," she guessed.

She was humoring him, he thought. "No, I hung an extra ornament."

It seemed as if every inch of the spruce tree was covered with ornaments. To notice just one was an impossible task.

"I'm afraid I don't—" And then she stopped. Because she suddenly did notice. In the center of the tree, just at her eye level, there was a dark blue velvet box. It was just sitting on a branch, between Cinderella dancing with her prince and Tinker Bell preening over a mirror at her feet.

Her heart stopped beating for a second. And then launched into double time. Laurel held her breath as she reached into the tree and drew out the box.

"Can I open it?" she asked in a whisper.

"You'd better."

Pressing her lips together, she raised the lid and for the second time in as many seconds, her breath halted.

The lights from the Christmas tree skimmed along the multiple surfaces of the pear-shaped diamond ring. As she tried to take the ring out, her hand trembled. Badly.

"Here, let me," Trent urged, taking the ring out of its box and then slipping it on her finger. "There, now, it's official. We're engaged," he told her. Just then, the doorbell rang. "Looks like the first wave is here," he said.

"They can wait," Laurel told him, wrapping her arms around his neck a heartbeat before she kissed him.

He grinned, applauding her. “Now you’re learning.” And then his lips met hers and all words were temporarily tabled.

* * * * *

Silhouette Desire kicks off 2009 with
MAN OF THE MONTH, *a yearlong program featuring incredible heroes by stellar authors.*

When Navy SEAL Hunter Cabot returns home for some much-needed R & R, he discovers he's a married man. There's just one problem: he's never met his "bride."

Enjoy this sneak peek at Maureen Child's
AN OFFICER AND A MILLIONAIRE.
Available January 2009 from Silhouette Desire.

One

Hunter Cabot, Navy SEAL, had a healing bullet wound in his side, thirty days' leave and, apparently, a wife he'd never met.

On the drive into his hometown of Springville, California, he stopped for gas at Charlie Evans's service station. That's where the trouble started.

"Hunter! Man, it's good to see you! Margie didn't tell us you were coming home."

"Margie?" Hunter leaned back against the front fender of his black pickup truck and winced as his side gave a small twinge of pain. Silently then, he watched as the man he'd known since high school filled his tank.

Charlie grinned, shook his head and pumped gas. "Guess your wife was lookin' for a little 'alone' time with you, huh?"

"My—" Hunter couldn't even say the word. *Wife?* He didn't have a wife. "Look, Charlie…"

"Don't blame her, of course," his friend said with a wink as he finished up and put the gas cap back on. "You being gone all the time with the SEALs must be hard on the ol' love life."

He'd never had any complaints, Hunter thought, frowning at the man still talking a mile a minute. "What're you—"

"Bet Margie's anxious to see you. She told us all about that R & R trip you two took to Bali." Charlie's dark brown eyebrows lifted and wiggled.

"Charlie…"

"Hey, it's okay, you don't have to say a thing, man."

What the hell could he say? Hunter shook his head, paid for his gas and as he left, told himself Charlie was just losing it. Maybe the guy had been smelling gas fumes too long.

But as it turned out, it wasn't just Charlie. Stopped at a red light on Main Street, Hunter glanced out his window to smile at Mrs. Harker, his second-grade teacher who was now at least a hundred years old. In the middle of the crosswalk, the old lady stopped and shouted, "Hunter Cabot, you've got yourself a wonderful wife. I hope you appreciate her."

Scowling now, he only nodded at the old woman—the only teacher who'd ever scared the crap out of him. What the hell was going on here? Was everyone but him nuts?

His temper beginning to boil, he put up with a few more comments about his "wife" on the drive through town before finally pulling into the wide, circular drive leading to the Cabot mansion. Hunter didn't have a clue what was going on, but he planned to get to the bottom of it. Fast.

He grabbed his duffel bag, stalked into the house and paid no attention to the housekeeper, who ran at him, fluttering both hands. "Mr. Hunter!"

"Sorry, Sophie," he called out over his shoulder as he took the stairs two at a time. "Need a shower, then we'll talk."

He marched down the long, carpeted hallway to the rooms that were always kept ready for him. In his suite, Hunter tossed the duffel down and stopped dead. The shower in his bathroom was running. His *wife?*

Anger and curiosity boiled in his gut, creating a churning mass that had him moving forward without even thinking about it. He opened the bathroom door to a wall of steam and the sound of a woman singing—off-key. Margie, no doubt.

Well, if she was his wife... Hunter walked across the room, yanked the shower door open and stared in at a curvy, naked, temptingly wet woman.

She whirled to face him, slapping her arms across her naked body while she gave a short, terrified scream.

Hunter smiled. "Hi, honey. I'm home."

* * * * *

Be sure to look for

AN OFFICER AND A MILLIONAIRE

by USA TODAY *bestselling author Maureen Child.*

Available January 2009 from Silhouette Desire.

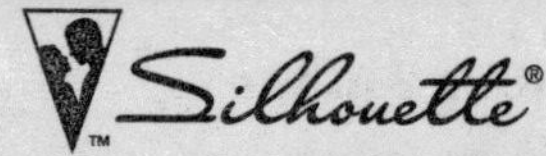

SPECIAL EDITION®

COMING NEXT MONTH

#1945 THE STRANGER AND TESSA JONES—
Christine Rimmer
Bravo Family Ties
The Bravos meet the Jones Gang as two of Christine Rimmer's famous Special Edition families come together in one very special book. Snowed in with an amnesiac stranger during a freak blizzard, Tessa Jones soon finds out her guest is none other than heartbreaker Ash Bravo. And that's when things really heat up....

#1946 PLAIN JANE AND THE PLAYBOY—Marie Ferrarella
Fortunes of Texas: Return to Red Rock
To kill time at a New Year's party, playboy Jorge Mendoza shows the host's teenage son how to woo the ladies. The random target of Jorge's charms: wallflower Jane Gilliam. But with one kiss at midnight, introverted Jane turns the tables on this would-be Casanova, as the commitment-phobe falls for her hook, line and sinker!

#1947 COWBOY TO THE RESCUE—Stella Bagwell
Men of the West
Hired to investigate the mysterious death of the Sandbur Ranch matriarch's late husband, private investigator Christina Logan enlists the help of cowboy-to-the-core Lex Saddler, Sandbur's youngest—and singlest—scion. Together, they find the truth...and each other.

#1948 REINING IN THE RANCHER—Karen Templeton
Wed in the West
Horse breeder Johnny Griego is blindsided by the news—both his ex-girlfriend Thea Benedict *and* his teenage daughter are pregnant. Never one to shirk responsibility, Johnny does the right thing and proposes to Thea. But Thea wants happily-ever-after, not a mere marriage of convenience. Can she rein in the rancher enough to have both?

#1949 SINGLE MOM SEEKS...—Teresa Hill
All newly divorced Lily Tanner wants is a safe, happy life with her two adorable daughters. Until hunky FBI agent Nick Malone moves in next door with his orphaned nephew. Now the pretty single mom's single days just might be numbered....

#1950 I STILL DO—Christie Ridgway
During a chance reunion in Vegas, former childhood sweethearts Will Dailey and Emily Garner let loose a little and make good on an old pledge—to wed each other if they weren't otherwise taken by age thirty! But in the cold light of day, the firefighter and librarian's quickie marriage doesn't seem like such a bright idea. Would their whim last a lifetime?